The FRIENDSHIP BOOK

of Francis Gay

D. C. THOMSON & CO., LTD.
London Glasgow Manchester Dundee

A Thought
For Each Day
In 2004

Laughter is like a ray of sunshine,
but friendship is the rainbow.

SHADOW OF THE CROSS

January

THURSDAY — JANUARY 1.

NEW YEAR

THE snowdrop and its message
Brings hope within each heart.
First bloom within the season,
Fresh aims for New Year's start.
Its struggle for survival
Inspiring to behold,
As with triumphant flourish
Its beauty will unfold.
Though Winter days of challenge
Are those we struggle through;
The snowdrop leads us forward —
Our resolutions, too!

Elizabeth Gozney.

FRIDAY — JANUARY 2.

I HAVE often been asked why this is called "The Friendship Book".

Well, many of my friends are in it, scattered through the pages. But of course there is more than that, for I like to think that everyone who reads it is a friend, too.

I will never know how many friends I have, and neither will you, but isn't it good to know they are there?

SATURDAY — JANUARY 3.

HERE is a happy, looking-ahead thought for the beginning of this new year from the pen of Robert Louis Stevenson:

Sing a song of seasons!
Something bright in all.
Flowers in the Summer,
Fires in the Fall.

Our old friend Mary thought you would like this little verse; she does, and has written it in her scrapbook.

SUNDAY — JANUARY 4.

AND Moses said unto them, Stand still, and I will hear what the Lord will command concerning you.

Numbers 9:8

MONDAY — JANUARY 5.

MARION is the headteacher of an infant school, and is dedicated to her job. But listening to her talking about some of the things which have happened to her, I couldn't help but marvel at how she manages to keep so calm and good humoured.

"Well, it's not always easy, Francis," she admitted. "But I try to remember the words of Eugene Delacroix. He said that, 'One is a master only when one brings to things the patience to which they are entitled'."

No wonder Marion is so good at her job — her philosophy is one which we might all benefit from remembering.

TUESDAY — JANUARY 6.

A SUITABLY seasonable snippet to share today from Great-Aunt Louisa's diary:

"January 6th — Received a small surprise parcel this morning from Peter and Helen in India. Inside was a soft silk scarf in a blend of beautiful Eastern colours, and a card wishing me 'Lovely, lasting peace of mind, sweet delight of human kind', and health and happiness."

Surely the best of wishes, which I in turn wish all my friends.

WEDNESDAY — JANUARY 7.

I ONCE rescued a magnificent golden dragonfly from a church pew where it had become entangled in spiders' webs. It was feebly trying to free its wings and legs. In a few seconds I had pulled away the strands, allowing it to rise up once again into the freedom of the Sunday morning air.

It made me think about myself, and about all of us. Here was this powerful creature of intricate beauty left unable to fly because of a few sticky threads. Its whole life was paralysed.

How often we become buried in darkness and depression because of one insignificant worry or frustration! The angrier we become the less able we are to escape. Eventually we cannot move any more, stuck in our own misery. But if we choose to let go, to refuse to allow ourselves to be trapped in self-pity, we'll be free to move on, and to be healed.

STEADFAST

THURSDAY — JANUARY 8.

VISITING a friend, the Lady of the House and I found Ethel busy rearranging her display cabinet. It was full of fascinating objects, a collection from her own lifetime and that of her parents before her.

At the back was a greetings card, truly a family treasure, for it was from an age when the fronts were delicately made to resemble lace-edged frames. Within the framework of this card was a delightful flower painting.

Ethel handed it to us to examine more closely. Carefully handwritten was a blessing, as relevant today as it was then:

"May the blessing of God attend thee, and the sun of Glory shine increasingly around thy paths."

FRIDAY — JANUARY 9.

IT is now two decades since the well-known pianist Artur Rubinstein died after a lifetime of giving immense pleasure to many people by his exquisite musical interpretations, especially of classical music.

One woman, who was a 12-year-old at the time, was entranced by the maestro's playing, and hoped to obtain the great man's autograph, although she had heard him say that as his hands were invariably tired after a concert, he couldn't write.

Smilingly, she approached the renowned pianist and said, "I know your fingers must be tired, sir; but so are mine — from clapping."

She got her treasured autograph.

SATURDAY — JANUARY 10.

"LOSE your temper and you lose your pride." I once heard that said and since then I have collected other sayings on the subject. Here are some:

"Everything you do in anger will be found to have been done wrong."

"Anger begins in folly and ends in repentance."

"Anger blows out the lamp of the mind."

"Anger today, tears tomorrow."

An American friend once told me, "I once lost my temper — and I'm glad to say I never found it again!"

SUNDAY — JANUARY 11.

FOR the Lord your God is God of gods, and Lord of lords, a great god. Deuteronomy 10:17

MONDAY — JANUARY 12.

JACK and Bert have been friends for many years. Now that they are both retired they often go for long walks together or visit their local pub for a drink. They have very different views about current affairs and sport, for example, so their conversation can become quite lively, to put it mildly.

"What I like most about Bert," says Jack, "is that he agrees to disagree without becoming disagreeable. He's a real friend."

Jack feels much the same about Bert. It's a good recipe for friendship.

COSY CORNER

TUESDAY — JANUARY 13.

YOU'LL know the phrase "down in the dumps", I'm sure, and most of us have felt like that at some time or another. One cure that always seems to work wonders is to talk to a friend. It's a great feeling to know that you can call on good friends when you need a bit of encouragement.

They can inspire us to do things we never thought possible — to tackle a difficult task, to try the unknown. We can seldom, if ever, enjoy a happy lifestyle if we avoid meeting and talking to friends. The writer and humanitarian Pearl S. Buck once said that the person who tries to live alone will not succeed.

"The heart withers," she wrote, "if it does not answer another heart. The mind shrinks away if it hears only the echoes of your own thoughts and finds no other inspiration."

Words worth remembering in a world that needs friendship.

WEDNESDAY — JANUARY 14.

A NEIGHBOUR of ours, Arnold, has been telling us that when he was a child it was quite common, when making promises, to say, "I will, I promise, on my honour."

Nowadays when he looks through the New Year's Honours List, he admires those who are chosen, yet adds, "The important thing is not so much whether we're in the Honours but whether there is honour in us."

THURSDAY— JANUARY 15.

"SHE means well." How often we hear that said of someone. I remember the phrase was once used to describe a certain lady to a stranger who did not know her.

The response has remained in my mind ever since: "Yes, but does she do well?"

For that's what really matters, isn't it?

FRIDAY — JANUARY 16.

MUSEUMS have changed. They are no longer the dark, dusty, and sometime dull places they perhaps used to be.

At Bradford a 19th-century school has been uprooted and rebuilt at the industrial museum. Schoolchildren enjoy visiting it, and the female pupils especially love sitting at the desks where their great-great-grandparents sat. They work at embroidery, while they listen to the story of how children worked in the mills during the morning and then went to school in the afternoon.

Something very special happens at this museum, too. Elderly people who suffer from loss of memory are brought along to these classes hoping that this will improve their wellbeing, even if just for a time. Curators, doctors and children have learned how to work together for others.

There are always some situations where an imaginative idea can help others who are ill or in distress. So if we have an idea — we shouldn't just sit and dream about it!

SATURDAY — JANUARY 17.

TODAY, as you go to work or out to enjoy leisure time, you are sure to hear people talking. Conversation and comment are never in short supply. The things that people say can, at various times, be cheerful or sad, wise or foolish, depressing or inspiring.

Writers have given us many fine examples of this, and none more so than a respected American journalist and editor, William Allen White (1868-1944), who created many distinctive quotes on life and living as he edited his small-town newspaper, the Emporia Gazette.

Here is one of his best-known: "I do not fear tomorrow, for I have seen yesterday — and I love today."

Inspiring words, don't you agree?

SUNDAY — JANUARY 18.

THE things which are impossible with men are possible with God.

Luke 18:27

MONDAY — JANUARY 19.

WE all like to think we can make a difference in the world and we all have different ways of going about it. The truth is, there is only one way. What is it? The secret is in this simple advice:

To leave footprints in the sands of time, wear working shoes.

TUESDAY — JANUARY 20.

A FRIEND was discussing the virtues of early retirement at a party. The pros and the cons were leading to lots of lively debate.

Then, suddenly, the value of age and experience came right into focus when one of our group, a lady in her late 80s, reminded us:

Actor George Burns won his first Oscar at 80.

Grandma Moses painted her first picture when she was past 80. After that she completed over 1500 paintings, and 25 per cent. of those were produced when she was past 100.

Michelangelo was 71 when he painted the Sistine Chapel.

Physician and humanitarian Albert Schweitzer was still performing operations in his African hospital at 89.

I need hardly add that our spirited debate ended with a decisive vote for the get-up-and-go spirit of our senior citizens!

WEDNESDAY — JANUARY 21.

IN his autobiography Howard Spring mentions a carpenter who was making a shelf for the Springs' home. On its completion the craftsman remarked, "I offer it up" as he placed the shelf in position.

Several years later, an acquaintance told me that the phrase was still used by her builder husband after he'd completed some work. She commented that it was surely a lovely thought and an apt phrase to pass on.

WINTER BLANKET

THURSDAY — JANUARY 22.

THE celebrated Irish writer and playwright George Bernard Shaw is probably best known by filmgoers as well as theatre audiences for his comedy-drama "Pygmalion", a great success on stage and screen as "My Fair Lady".

However, you have only to study the long list of writings to realise that this witty and eloquent man from Dublin has given us countless gems of thought and wisdom. Here is a memorable example:

"Life is no brief candle to me. It is like a splendid torch which I have got hold of for a moment, and I want to make it burn as bright as possible before I hand it on to future generations."

FRIDAY — JANUARY 23.

AGNES' garden was looking rather bleak in the Winter months. There had been a lot of rain and the trees and shrubs looked sad and bedraggled, but she told me she still got a lot of pleasure from it.

"I follow my father's advice," she said. "He used to tell me I should always put a bird table where it can be seen from the kitchen window. That way, the garden is never empty."

Sure enough, even though there were no flowers, the birds fluttering down to feed at the table and then flying off to perch on a nearby branch meant that, even in Winter, Agnes' garden was always alive.

SATURDAY — JANUARY 24.

I WONDER if you know these well-known lines.

Man's inhumanity to Man,
Makes countless thousands mourn.

Most of us, I think, would agree with the sentiments of these words, written by one of the world's best-loved poets and songwriters. He was Robert Burns, born in a humble cottage at Alloway in Ayrshire on 25th January 1759.

Robert, with the unforgettable dark eyes, was a tenant farmer and exciseman, an accomplished letter writer and above all, a poet and collector and writer of Scots songs. His poems and songs are rich in their many observations of humanity, humour and wisdom. He could express in words and song what people feel in their hearts, and perhaps that is why his poetry continues to be read and recited. He engraved these words on a window of his Ellisland farmhouse:

An honest man's the noblest work of God.

Words which, I am sure, will find a sympathetic echo in many hearts.

SUNDAY — JANUARY 25.

AND this is life eternal, that they might know thee the only true God, and Jesus Christ, whom thou hast sent.

John 17:3

MONDAY — JANUARY 26.

TREAT happiness like marmalade. Spread it well. There's plenty to go round!

TUESDAY — JANUARY 27.

THE time goes by so swiftly, Lord,
The months all slip away,
And as I turn the calendar
This little prayer I pray —
"Don't let me waste a day."

The Springtime is so beautiful,
Bright April, lovely May,
With blossom trees and flower shows
A wonderful display —
"Don't let me waste a day."

The harvest time, the Autumn time
Blue skies may turn to grey,
And though the Winter follows soon
It, too, will slip away —
"Don't let me waste a day."

Iris Hesselden.

WEDNESDAY — JANUARY 28.

IN these days of rush and hurry, we often seem to live in a world where the value of our lives can, it appears, only be measured against our salary, our status, the number of tasks undertaken and accomplished.

It was refreshing, therefore, to come across an entirely different attitude in this quote from the pen of poet Emily Dickinson: "To live," she wrote, "is so startling it leaves little time for anything else."

We should never be so busy that we miss out on the sheer wonder of being alive.

THURSDAY — JANUARY 29.

FRIENDS were once talking about how they would miss a good friend who had gone to live many miles away.

"George," somebody remarked, "is positive in all he does and says, but what we like most about him is that he always has that happy twinkle in his eye."

"That happy twinkle!" Now, that speaks for itself. You either have it or you don't, but when it is there, the person adds a sparkle to the day.

FRIDAY — JANUARY 30.

SOMETIMES we try to accomplish something too quickly, then wonder why we are not succeeding. When I find myself in danger of doing this I think of these lines I heard years ago:

Yard by yard, all tasks are hard.
Inch by inch, they're all a cinch!

SATURDAY— JANUARY 31.

TAKE five minutes here and there
Within the busy day,
Make a special quiet time
To meditate and pray.
When we let go and turn to God
The spirit is refreshed,
We find that we are comforted
Calmed, and soothed, and blessed.

Kathleen Gillum.

February

SUNDAY — FEBRUARY 1.

THOU shalt be perfect with the Lord thy God.

Deuteronomy 18:13

MONDAY — FEBRUARY 2.

WHILE out walking one day with the Lady of the House we were caught in a heavy shower. We were glad to be offered shelter by our friend Phyllis. "What atrocious weather!" I said.

Always the philosopher, Phyllis replied, "It has its advantages, you know. It gives me the chance to chat with old friends, and it reminds me of a story I once read." Phyllis is famed for her stories, which always make their point.

This tale concerned a heavy fall of snow which made it difficult for people to get about. Children at a local school had been told to stay at home, although improved conditions the next morning meant that school could re-open. An enthusiastic teacher said that she hoped her young charges had passed the time at home profitably.

"What did you do, Nicholas?" she asked one boy. The prompt and honest reply came at once: "Please, Miss, I prayed for more snow for today!"

TUESDAY — FEBRUARY 3.

THE DOOR OF PRAYER

WHEN you feel you are forgotten
And no-one seems to care,
Close the door on all your trouble
And open one in prayer.
Let the light and love surround you
And leave the world behind,
And with the healing gift of prayer
Discover peace of mind.

When your rocky road seems endless
Without a bend or turn,
Light a candle in the darkness
And watch it gently burn.
Seek the hidden strength within you
And find new courage there,
Close the door on all your trouble
And open one in prayer.

Iris Hesselden.

WEDNESDAY — FEBRUARY 4.

ERIC SYKES, the much-loved comedian, became deaf and almost blind, yet kept on working and even managed to act in plays in London's West End as well as appearing on the big screen.

He once said that he looked on his infirmities as no more than hiccups. "In this life you either walk with your head up or you walk with it down. I'm keeping mine up!"

A great example to follow.

WATER COLOURS

THURSDAY — FEBRUARY 5.

VISITORS to York's famous Castle Museum may remember that when it was a prison, a visiting robin inspired James Montgomery, the writer and poet, to praise the bird by composing a verse.

Montgomery had been imprisoned for his religious and semi-political beliefs, and the only visitor to cheer his day was a robin. No wonder he wrote of his feathered friend:

Welcome, pretty little stranger
Welcome to my lone retreat,
Robin. How I envy thee
Happy child of liberty.

The robin must have brought good tidings, too, for not long afterwards James Montgomery was released from prison.

FRIDAY — FEBRUARY 6.

ONE of our local churches put up a series of sayings on its noticeboard about money. The clergyman told his congregation, "No, they are not aimed at enlarging the church collection, but to encourage our thinking." Here are some of them:

You will never find Happiness quoted on the Stock Exchange.

God has invested everything in you. Are you showing any interest?

Let us make the most of ourselves, not the most for ourselves. Then we will be truly rich.

SATURDAY — FEBRUARY 7.

DORIS, a youthful 89-year-old, was looking back on a lifetime of meeting people of many types in many circumstances.

"Some people come into our lives and quickly go," she said. "Some move our souls to dance, and awaken us to new understanding with the passing whisper of their wisdom. Others make the sky more beautiful to gaze upon. They stay in our lives for a while, leave footprints on our hearts. And we are never, ever the same again."

A thought from Doris that is well worth considering.

SUNDAY — FEBRUARY 8.

AND many wonders and signs were done by the apostles. And all that believed were together, and had all things common.

Acts 2:43-4

MONDAY — FEBRUARY 9.

I WANT you to take a tip today from Hippocrates, the physician who lived on the Greek island of Kos and is famous as "The Father Of Medicine". His recipe for good health was — "Walking is man's best medicine."

How true! A modern-day doctor friend says a walk can give all of us "a truly peaceful feeling".

"Walk slowly with no goal in mind," Hippocrates advises. "Keep good posture and smile as you walk."

One of the simplest recipes for good health, and over 2000 years old!

TUESDAY — FEBRUARY 10.

MOTHER TERESA has given us many fine thoughts, but this one, I think, ranks among her best:

Life is an opportunity, benefit from it.
Life is beauty, admire it.
Life is bliss, taste it.
Life is a dream, realise it.
Life is a challenge, meet it.
Life is a duty, complete it.
Life is a game, play it.
Life is a promise, fulfil it.
Life is sorrow, overcome it.
Life is a song, sing it.
Life is a struggle, accept it.
Life is a tragedy, confront it.
Life is an adventure, dare it.
Life is luck, make it.
Life is too precious, do not destroy it.
Life is life, fight for it.

WEDNESDAY — FEBRUARY 11.

WHAT do you know about Napoleon Bonaparte? Of course there were the famous battles he fought, and his long years of exile but what I like to remember him for is that he urged the people of France to plant trees along the roadsides to give shade for his troops and other travellers under the hot sun.

Rows of trees are still part of the French landscape today. Not a bad legacy to leave your country.

THURSDAY — FEBRUARY 12.

A FRIEND had just returned from holiday. "Did you have a good time?" I asked.

"We've had a lovely break, thanks," he replied. "It was a delightful place, the weather was lovely and, as for the hotel, it was comfortable, served good food and it had a feature which, for me, is the mark of a really good hotel — in every bedroom guests find a copy of the Gideons' Bible."

I have always admired the Gideons, who donate Bibles like this. When you are far from home it's amazing what comfort and relaxation you can get from dipping into one of their Bibles. For those who find little time to study the Bible, they might like to fill a few minutes every so often with a perusal of the Good Book.

A Gideons' Bible adds a special touch to a home from home.

FRIDAY — FEBRUARY 13.

THE Lady of the House shares my love of literature. She was browsing in a volume of Shakespeare's plays one day when she suddenly exclaimed, "That's very true!" She had been looking at "King Henry IV" and saw these lines, spoken by Prince Henry:

"If all the year were playing holidays, to sport would be as tedious as to work." We don't know if Shakespeare knew the saying about all work and no play making Jack a dull boy, but he certainly knew the reverse is true.

SATURDAY — FEBRUARY 14.

IF you choose roses for your loved one today, you are continuing a truly romantic tradition. From the time of Solomon a rose has been the flower most closely linked to love and friendship.

Red roses say: "I Love You" and also stand for respect and courage. Yellow roses signify joy, gladness and friendship.

In the Victorian age bashful suitors offered gifts of roses to convey the depth of their feelings. Robert Burns immortalised the flower, too:

O, my Luve's like a red, red rose,
That's newly sprung in June.
O, my Luve is like a melodie
That's sweetly play'd in tune.

Go back centuries, however, and we find a tribute just as glowing. "True fragrance," says an old Chinese proverb, "will always cling to the hand that gives you roses."

SUNDAY — FEBRUARY 15.

AND Jesus, when he was baptised, went up straightway out of the water: and, lo, the heavens were opened unto him, and he saw the Spirit of God descending like a dove, and lighting upon him.

Matthew 3:16

MONDAY — FEBRUARY 16.

COURAGE doesn't always roar. Sometimes courage is the little voice at the end of the day that says: "I'll try again tomorrow."

TUESDAY — FEBRUARY 17.

HAVE you ever noticed how so many different things in life can be seen as good or bad simply depending upon the way we view them?

When Elizabeth found herself being routinely woken at four o'clock by the dawn chorus, she was not at all happy. Much as she loved songbirds, she soon began to dread the regular disturbance.

But then, one day it occurred to her that if she couldn't avoid the problem, she might just as well try looking at it from a different angle. Next time, instead of lying there fretting about the rather rude awakening she decided to try to enjoy the concert, and even to attempt to identify the individual performers.

"And, do you know, it has worked!" she told me triumphantly. "Even though it's true that I don't always get back to sleep immediately, now I don't mind lying awake nearly so much!"

Such a minor shift of attitude, but such a major improvement.

WEDNESDAY — FEBRUARY 18.

HERE is one of the best descriptions of friendship I have come upon:

"The glory of friendship is not the outstretched hand, nor the kindly smile, nor the joy of companionship. It is the spiritual inspiration that comes to you when you discover that someone else believes in you and is willing to trust you with their friendship."

THURSDAY — FEBRUARY 19.

A CORRESPONDENT has passed on to me an item from his church magazine. It was headed "Life's Little Instructions":

Keep it simple.
Be forgiving of yourself and others.
Compliment three people every day.
Never waste an opportunity to let someone know you love them.
Become the most positive and enthusiastic person you know.

Good advice, surely.

FRIDAY — FEBRUARY 20.

JANE, who had just celebrated her seventy-third birthday, told her grandchildren that she had never learnt to swim, even though it was something she had always wanted to do. They said, "Go on, Granny, go to swimming lessons!" And she did.

She was very nervous at the first lesson. The instructor told his class, "Last year one man had progressed sufficiently to attempt swimming the length of this pool. He swam halfway but then thought he couldn't make it to the end, so he turned round and swam back!"

I wonder if that story was really true, but anyway, it spurred Jane on. By the end of the ten-session course she could swim lengths confidently and was presented with a certificate.

Let's all try to accomplish something new — we'll feel such a sense of achievement.

SATURDAY— FEBRUARY 21.

HENRY had just come back from the optician's where he'd been told he needed stronger spectacles.

"Oh, well," he told me philosophically, "if I end up like my grandad, I shan't do too badly. He never did have good vision, but there were three things that he never lost sight of. He could always see the beauty in the world, the funny side of life, and the good within people."

Not a bad list, I think!

SUNDAY — FEBRUARY 22.

AND Jesus said, I am: and ye shall see the Son of man sitting on the right hand of power, and coming in the clouds of heaven. Mark 14:62

MONDAY — FEBRUARY 23.

THESE simple lines are from a hymn for children:

Think of a world without any flowers,
Think of a world without any trees,
Think of a sky without any sunshine,
Think of the air without any breeze.

Think of a world without any animals,
Think of a field without any herd,
Think of a stream without any fishes,
Think of a dawn without any bird.

Yes, it makes you think, doesn't it? And I don't know about you, but it makes me grateful.

THE DOOR IS
ALWAYS OPEN

TUESDAY— FEBRUARY 24

WHEN I'm in company, I often remind myself of how Calvin Coolidge, a former President of the USA, once said: "It takes a great man to be a good listener."

The writer Ernest Hemingway also put it neatly: "I have learned a great deal from listening carefully. Most people never listen."

Singer Pearl Bailey said that talking to someone who doesn't listen is "enough to tease the devil".

Everyone, I find, has either a problem or an achievement that he or she wants to talk about and they want to share it. Isn't it good, then, to try to be a better listener?

WEDNESDAY — FEBRUARY 25.

DONKEYS are patient, indomitable creatures who have served mankind for centuries.

G. K. Chesterton wrote a memorable little poem "The Donkey" and you may recall that it ends: "For I too had my hour; one far fierce hour and sweet: there was a shout about my ears, and palms before my feet."

This is a message repeated many times in Scripture where the importance of these gentle and loyal animals has never been forgotten.

THURSDAY — FEBRUARY 26.

WHEN you have happiness, don't hoard it. The more of it you give away, the more you'll still have.

FRIDAY — FEBRUARY 27.

ANTONY was a celebrated photographer who specialised in studio portraits. Not, as you might expect, glamorous young people but older folk.

He explained that, for him, there was a beauty in the faces of men and women that always inspired him.

"A young face is still a blank page," he used to say. "An old face, with all its lines and wrinkles, is a whole book."

SATURDAY — FEBRUARY 28.

ISN'T it curious how the same thing is seen by different people in different ways? Jim and his son went fishing one day and, like many another angler, they returned home empty-handed.

Years later, after the two had both died, someone looked through their diaries — and found contrasting entries for that same day. Jim had written: "Caught nothing. Another wasted day." His son, however, had written: "Today I went fishing with my dad. It was the best day of my life."

Quality time had enriched his day and given him something he could be thankful for.

SUNDAY — FEBRUARY 29.

AND when he saw their faith, he said unto him, Man, thy sins are forgiven thee.

Luke 5:20

March

MONDAY — MARCH 1.

EARLY Spring and sleeps the bud
Below the blanket soil.
Look closely and we surely see
The fruit of Nature's toil,
Confetti showers of crocus
Green guards of honour stand,
Proud to welcome Springtime
Nature's alarm-call to the land.

Katy Clarke.

TUESDAY — MARCH 2.

"OH dear," said the traveller as he arrived at the airport. "I do wish I'd thought to pack the piano — because that's where I've left my ticket!"

Yes, it's an old joke but it always makes me smile, and perhaps even more importantly, reminds us what a valuable asset a sense of humour is.

We can never hope to walk through the world avoiding all life's banana skins, but by treating such mishaps with humour we can often help ourselves to cope better.

A sense of humour is one thing that can never be left on the piano!

WEDNESDAY — MARCH 3.

WHEN Angela was a child, few would have held much hope for her chances of success. She was born into a large family living in a poor locality, and when she struggled with schoolwork, neither parents nor teachers seemed to have much extra time to help.

However, what Angela did have was a wonderful neighbour. Every evening she would invite the child round and listen to her read and count, praising her efforts with genuine enthusiasm.

Today Angela is a teacher herself, and credits much of her achievement to her kindly neighbour. "It made all the difference," she said. "Her belief in me made me believe in myself, so I stopped being frightened by lessons and started to see them as something I could tackle and win. Now I try to pass on that feeling of confidence to my own pupils."

I'm sure Angela's neighbour would have reckoned that to be the very best kind of thank-you.

THURSDAY — MARCH 4.

WORDS, it has been said, should be chosen with great care. As my friend Duncan observed, "The wisest person is the one who, having nothing to say, stays clear of giving wordy evidence of the fact."

I agree. May I adapt a useful slogan from the highway and say: "Drive your thoughts with care."

FRIDAY — MARCH 5.

"LIFE is not all beer and skittles. The inherent tragedy of things works itself out from white to black and blacker, and the poor things of a day look ruefully on. Does it shake my cast-iron faith? I cannot say it does, I believe in an ultimate decency of things."

Robert Louis Stevenson wrote these words in 1893 and aren't they uplifting ones to read today when life may seem less than bright? A courageous statement of faith, written by a man who was in his short life no stranger to adversity and recurring illness.

As a "teller of tales" this Edinburgh-born writer left us a legacy of classic adventure stories, such as "Kidnapped" and "Treasure Island" and his much-loved "A Child's Garden Of Verses". He died on the island of Samoa in 1894.

SATURDAY — MARCH 6.

JO was telling us about the friends she has made since she came to live in our neighbourhood. The Lady of the House and I asked, "What makes a good friend?"

Jo thought for a moment, then said, "It's someone who makes a difference to your life for the better." Then she added, "It's the person who makes a short telephone call to say 'Hi', the person who quietens your fears, raises your spirits and, most important of all, gently tells you his or her true feelings about a problem when you need to hear it."

SUNDAY — MARCH 7.

AND Jesus answered and said unto him, What wilt thou that I should do unto thee? The blind man said unto him, Lord, that I might receive my sight.
Mark 10:51

MONDAY — MARCH 8.

OUR friend Ian enjoys those television programmes in which well-known artists talk about their skills and inspiration. One day, he watched an interesting one in which Yorkshire artist Ashley Jackson was speaking about his Spanish grandmother with whom he had much in common.

Both had unhappy childhoods which helped, no doubt, to form their characters. She also taught him a most important lesson for an artist — to observe things acutely. As Ashley wisely said, "A lot of us have eyesight, but few of us have vision."

There is always so much more to see in the world if only we look for it, whether we are artists or not.

TUESDAY — MARCH 9.

AFTER THE WINTER

LIFT up your head, to the sun's warming rays,
Rejoice in the light and the lengthening days,
The Springtime is touching the path that
you tread
With hope for the future, so lift up your head.

Iris Hesselden.

WEDNESDAY — MARCH 10.

AN aunt and uncle of the popular Scottish singer Robert Wilson, after a stimulating journey from New York to Scotland, sent their nephew a telegram in rhyme, saying how much they had enjoyed the trip.

Robert took it as a challenge, popped into the nearest post office, grabbed a bunch of telegram forms and, on the back, wrote a message. He sent it off by wire to reach Uncle John and Aunt Jean aboard the *Queen Mary* as they sailed back across the Atlantic.

Haste ye back, We lo'e ye dearly,
Call again, you're welcome here,
May your days be free from sorrow,
And your friends be ever near.

Some time later Robert recorded the words in song, and they became the famous signature-tune of the television series "The White Heather Club".

If you want to say thank you to someone, why not put your words down on paper now? And they don't have to be in rhyme!

THURSDAY — MARCH 11.

THE busy city office where our friend Jean works is a truly happy place. A simple notice prominently displayed could well be the reason, she says. It advises:

"The Best Day is . . . Today!"

A challenging thought for this and every day of the year.

FRIDAY — MARCH 12.

A WEDDING at our church had sparked a discussion about the best present you could give a bride and groom.

It was our old friend Mary, however, who came up with the most interesting answer. "When I got married," she told us, "none of my friends had much money for gifts. So they got together to buy a large scrapbook and stuck in copies of all their favourite recipes, plus a snapshot of each contributor. I still have the book, all these years later. Not only has it inspired many an excellent meal — even better, every dish has been flavoured with happy memories."

An example of how friendship adds relish to life!

SATURDAY — MARCH 13.

THE Lady of the House had been to a talk about the early settlers who sailed from England to America on the Mayflower.

"It was interesting," she said, "but the speaker talked all evening about the Pilgrim Fathers. He never once spoke about the Pilgrim Mothers. They had just as hard a time of it, if not worse, and what is more they had to put up with the Pilgrim Fathers!"

SUNDAY — MARCH 14.

AND when the Lord saw her, he had compassion on her, and said unto her, Weep not.

Luke 7:13

MONDAY — MARCH 15.

I HAVE been given a book of quotations, many of which are new to me. I especially like this one from Mother Teresa:

"Let us always meet each other with a smile, for a smile is the beginning of love."

It reminded me of how a friend was feeling rather sad and lonely. One morning she decided she must do something to cheer herself up. She brushed her hair, put on lipstick, wore her best coat, then set off to town.

As she walked through the streets, she smiled at those she met, spoke to numerous people, including many she didn't know, and generally spread sunshine. Not everyone responded, of course, but she didn't give up, and by the time she returned home she felt much better — it was a turning point.

Whatever the burden, always try to reach out. You will find many who will respond. They, too, may be in need of reassurance and will feel so much better for having met you. Who knows, you may plant a seed of love in another lonely heart.

TUESDAY — MARCH 16.

ARE you easily hurt? Have there been times when an unfair remark has cut you to the quick? Next time, here's how to fight it.

It's simply a case of mind over matter — if you don't mind, it doesn't matter!

WEDNESDAY — MARCH 17.

THE wheatear is a perky little bird of the hills, coasts and open country. In the Highlands they used to call it the bird of St Patrick.

Why? Well, wheatears leave us for warmer climes in Autumn but people did not then know about migration and thought the birds slept till Spring under the ground. They believed the wheatears awoke to appear again to greet the morning of St Patrick's Day.

Aren't some of these old beliefs lovely?

THURSDAY — MARCH 18.

WHILE listening to the weather forecast, it occurred to me that we could have our own individual "Family Forecast". After all, we are rather like the weather, aren't we? A little unpredictable.

Perhaps it could go something like this: "There may be a slight depression early in the day, followed by a short but turbulent period. There should be a calmer spell mid-morning, but the afternoon could be changeable. Sunshine should return around tea-time. Evening will be quieter and the night should be still, with little or no disturbance. The outlook for the weekend: expect periods of intense activity and some quiet spells."

And for those of us who no longer rush around: "No storms in the foreseeable future. More sunlight on the distant horizon."

Have a nice day!

EARTH'S
TREASURE

FRIDAY — MARCH 19.

WILLIAM Shakespeare was surely right when he said:

All the world's a stage,
And all the men and women merely players.
They have their exits and entrances . . .

These words invite the question — what parts are we prepared to play in this grand production known as Life? Although we never know what may be waiting in the wings, if we allow ourselves to be up-staged by Gloom and Pessimism, that surely is a Tragedy.

SATURDAY — MARCH 20.

THERE'S a famous old saying that runs: "What goes around, comes around." Hearing a friend quoting these words, I realised just how much it revolves around the wonderful virtue of kindness. Here are two thoughts on that subject, both worth remembering:

"You cannot do a kindness too soon, for you never know how soon it will be too late."

Ralph Waldo Emerson.

"Wise sayings often fall on barren ground, but a kind word is never thrown away."

Sir Arthur Helps.

SUNDAY — MARCH 21.

HE that receiveth you receiveth me, and he that receiveth me receiveth him that sent me.

Matthew 10:40

MONDAY — MARCH 22.

ARE you a worrier? When I was young an old man used to say to me, "Never worry worry till worry worries you."

Of course, this isn't always so easy but one thing I have discovered is this: what seems like a huge worry in the middle of the night shrinks to nothing by breakfast time. As someone once said, "Worries that come by night fly by day."

"I have no worries," a friend once told me. "Or if I do, I don't know it!"

Another friend said, "Yes, I've had my worries, but I didn't keep any of 'em. I found they were no use to me so I just threw them away."

TUESDAY — MARCH 23.

HAVE you ever heard of Marion Wright Edelman? She is an American, born in South Carolina, who has devoted most of her life to improving the lives of disadvantaged children in her country — so successfully that she has won many honours and awards for her efforts.

The task must often have seemed overwhelming, but she has never allowed herself to be intimidated. "We must not," she said, "in trying to think about how we can make a big difference, ignore the small daily differences we can make."

It's an inspiring attitude. Next time I feel discouraged by a problem, I shall try to remember that even a small difference is always worth the making.

WEDNESDAY — MARCH 24.

FOR some days the weather had been decidedly indifferent, one cold wet day following another. "Typical British weather!" a neighbour grumbled.

Then Sunday morning dawned, warm and sunny; we enjoyed our walk to church. A smiling clergyman greeted us with the words, "Due to the weather I've changed the first hymn. Let us sing the one which begins, 'This is the day that the Lord has made, let us rejoice and be glad in it!' "

Days like that make you feel good to be alive, for we appreciate the sunshine more when it has been absent for a while. But as we were reminded in the sermon, even on the darkest of days the Lord is there, spreading His light on our darkness, if only we have eyes to see.

Better days will come if we have faith and confidence.

THURSDAY — MARCH 25.

A PROVERB states: "Only in winter do we know the pine and the cypress to be evergreen."

There are people we know who seem as substantial as an oak in full leaf, or as flattering as a maple in its Autumn colours. But, come a bad spell, they'll shrink to a mere skeleton of their former glory. True friends are the evergreens who will still be there to give shelter, whatever the weather.

FRIDAY — MARCH 26.

THROUGH THE SEASONS

GOD sends the seasons through the year
To bring His presence ever near,
And in the beauty of each day,
We feel new hopes along our way.
To light a smile within each face,
And step ahead with steadfast pace,
To put a Spring in every stride,
And Summer's promise at our side.

Elizabeth Gozney.

SATURDAY — MARCH 27.

HOW often have we heard the well-known performer's cry, "The show must go on!" Well, I once read an interesting story about the great opera singer, Cecilia Bartoli.

When rehearsing in Zurich for the part of Donna Elvira in Mozart's "Don Giovanni", she slipped and suffered a fracture. Later, she left hospital in a wheelchair and performed her part in the opera on crutches.

She declared, "It hurt horribly, but what could I do? I could not let everybody down."

Not only a great singer but a determined one!

SUNDAY — MARCH 28.

AND he said unto them, Where is your faith? And they being afraid wondered, saying one to another, What manner of man is this! for he commandeth even the winds and water, and they obey him.

Luke 8:25

CHILDREN'S HOUR

MONDAY— MARCH 29.

ARE you on any committees? Of course we need them in various organisations, but I rather sympathise with the man who said that the ideal committee was made up of himself as chairman and two other members in bed with flu.

Someone else once observed that if Christopher Columbus's trip had been planned by a committee his ship would still be tied up at the dock.

To round off, I love the description of a camel as a horse designed by a committee!

TUESDAY — MARCH 30.

A TEACHER I know has a good way of encouraging her pupils to appreciate modern inventions. Each week she sets aside a few minutes to discuss something they take for granted. It may be an electric light bulb, a ballpoint pen, a wrist-watch, even a toothbrush!

"They learn to look at these things with a fresh eye," she told me, "and to realise how lucky they are to have them."

It's a lesson we might all take to heart.

WEDNESDAY — MARCH 31.

THE medical students seemed to be stumped when the question was put to them: "What is the shinbone for?"

At last one bright spark raised his hand and offered, "Finding furniture in the dark?"

Ouch!

April

THURSDAY — APRIL 1.

IF you are ever tired of this world's burden of care and find no joy in the midst of all its pain, try waking early in the morning and listen to the dawn chorus. It begins with a single bird, often a thrush, and builds until a whole thatch of song fills the trees around, whether in city or country.

Listen to it, for it is a song of thanksgiving for the light, the Spring, the promise of a new day.

FRIDAY — APRIL 2.

I'M a firm believer that the simplest things in life can often bring as much pleasure as the most expensive treats. This little rhyme, composed by our friend Susan while relaxing after a long walk, promotes this view:

A pot of tea,
A home-made bun,
A garden chair,
Some dappled sun —
Such joys may not
Impress a king
But as for me,
They're just the thing!

SATURDAY — APRIL 3.

"WHAT are you giving up for Lent?" a friend once asked. Sometimes rather overlooked nowadays, we both began to recall the days when giving up some pleasure for Lent was almost a must.

The sermon the previous Sunday had reminded us of the origin of Lent, the Forty Days in the wilderness, days of concentrated thought for Our Lord. He emerged later, knowing why He was here and what He had to do — to point his disciples to God, to celebrate life by loving Him, loving ourselves and, above all, loving our neighbours.

We may sometimes neglect to give up much for Lent these days, but it's not a bad idea to think about those Forty Days, remembering His love, and trying to translate it into service for our friends and the community. Two thousand years on, the lesson of Lent is still relevant.

SUNDAY — APRIL 4.

THEN said Jesus to them again, Peace be unto you: as my Father hath sent me, even so send I you.

John 20:21

MONDAY — APRIL 5.

I'D like to share with you today this tip from a church notice-board, worth remembering should you find yourself awake in the middle of the night:

Can't sleep? Well, try counting your blessings.

TUESDAY — APRIL 6.

NO-ONE quite knows how cats purr. Scientists have tried to find out why, yet this expression of happiness remains shrouded in mystery. It's somehow comforting to know that there are things which haven't been explained, that this wonderful world in which we live still has its secrets.

After all, purring is a gift of love, and no matter how long we live on this earth, scientists will never be able to tell us exactly what or where love is inside us. Nor do we need to know — what matters is that we believe in it.

WEDNESDAY — APRIL 7.

IT was a breezy day when the Lady of the House decided to go into the back garden to plant a new shrub. Soon she was wishing that she had an extra pair of hands as she struggled in the wind. Then, around the corner of the house came our gardener friend Joe, who is always ready to lend a hand.

"Hello!" he greeted her. "I had a feeling you were going to need me today." And without more ado he picked up the spade.

"I was glad when Joe turned up," said the Lady of the House later.

"Yes," I agreed, "there's no doubt that many hands make light work, and it reminds me of something else I once read — 'a true friend is someone who comes in adversity without invitation'."

THURSDAY — APRIL 8.

YOU know, there is something about this time of year as we draw ever closer to Easter which always strikes me as being particularly special.

This is a time for thoughtfulness and reflection, and it never fails to bring to my mind those wonderful words of Psalm 46: "Be still, and know that I am God."

It's a loving reminder to us all, and worth keeping in our hearts, not just at this season of the year, but at any time when the demands of our world seem set to overwhelm us.

FRIDAY — APRIL 9.

FEELING a little down today? Nothing much happening in your world? Well, here's something I have learned over the years: if you can't do anything for yourself, do something for somebody else instead!

You may think it's too much of an effort, and why can't someone do something for you? Well, I understand how you might feel, but this approach does work. Supposing you're not very well, or you are housebound? Even then, you can perhaps write a card or a letter to someone and a phone call to someone lonely would be much appreciated.

If you are out shopping, give someone a greeting. Many people are desperately in need of one.

At the end of the day you will be surprised how much better you will feel, and tomorrow will be brighter for you — and others!

SATURDAY — APRIL 10.

IN the Hebrides people used to believe that the sun dances for joy on Easter Sunday. An old woman, Barbara Macphie, said she had once been fortunate enough to witness it.

She had climbed to the top of the island's highest hill to await the dawn. When the sun appeared, she said it was "dancing up and down in exultation."

Perhaps we can't share that vision with Barbara, but we can all share her joy this Easter.

SUNDAY — APRIL 11.

MARY Magdalene came and told the disciples that she had seen the Lord, and that he had spoken these things unto her.

John 20:18

MONDAY — APRIL 12.

WHEN the moon's no longer shining
And the road ahead is drear,
What a welcome in the distance
When a window light shines clear!
Though it is a house of strangers,
Friendly comfort spreads around,
Brings the warmth of kindly caring,
For the light of hope, is found.
Lone no longer, now the journey,
Going forth into the night;
God sends faith to walk beside you,
Leads you with His guiding light . . .

Elizabeth Gozney.

WHERE THE HEART IS

TUESDAY — APRIL 13.

HAS the Winter left you feeling your age? Shoulders drooping a little and a few wrinkles you hadn't noticed before appearing? Well, don't be downhearted. It's Spring and we should all start to perk up again soon.

I was feeling a bit lethargic one day, when I found this quotation: "Growing old is no more than a bad habit which a busy person has no time to form."

It seems to me we should put the Winter behind us and keep ourselves occupied. Write those letters, make those phone calls and, if possible, step out with a lighter tread.

Observe the world around you, enjoy the Spring. Go forward cheerfully!

WEDNESDAY — APRIL 14.

IT was a glorious morning — the forsythia was magnificent, the hedgerows were ablaze with broom and around every available tree trunk, the daffodils nodded their agreement in wonder at the God-given day.

Suddenly, the sky darkened, the heavens opened and all that could be seen and heard was sleet, driving rain and the drumming of hailstones. A different world? Yes, but even in such a bleak landscape, the heartening, warming sun-yellow of the forsythia, broom and daffodils lived on.

A bit like life itself, perhaps? No matter how dark our problems, there's always a chink of light to encourage us to keep on keeping on.

THURSDAY — APRIL 15.

SALLY is a great worker for charities — she never seems to waste a moment. When I remarked on this she smiled and said:

"As a girl I was always putting things off. One day I told my grandfather, 'I won't bother doing this now — there will be plenty of other days'.

"He looked at me and said quietly, 'Yes, Sally, but never again this day'."

Those wise words have shaped Sally's life.

FRIDAY — APRIL 16.

THE WAY OF PEACE

YOU look like my brother,
Why should we fight and kill?
And you look like my sister,
Loved and remembered still.
And all those other people,
Like some I used to know,
My childhood friends and absent friends
I lost so long ago.

If we are all one family
Why can't we seek and find,
A better understanding
With hope for all mankind?
You look like my brother,
Let friendship now increase,
And clasping hands around the world
We'll find the way of peace.

Iris Hesselden.

SATURDAY — APRIL 17.

THE Lady of the House and I were talking about useful inventions — not the big ones but the kind of everyday things we are all apt to take for granted.

I came up with shoelaces, spectacles and the screwdriver, while the Lady of the House suggested the comb, scissors and the safety-pin!

Little things perhaps, but all vitally important to our everyday lives.

SUNDAY — APRIL 18.

THEN they that gladly received his word were baptised: and the same day there were added unto them about three thousand souls.

Acts 2:41

MONDAY — APRIL 19.

THE Lady of the House's friend Enid arrived home from a picnic.

"Even though the weather wasn't perfect, we still enjoyed ourselves," she said. "Everyone brought something different to eat or drink, and we all shared whatever we had.

"In fact," she added, "it struck me that there's a lot of similarity between life and a picnic — we all bring different talents into the world, and the more we share them around, the better a time can be enjoyed by all."

Next time I hear someone grumble that life is no picnic, then perhaps I will suggest that we should all try harder to make it more so!

TUESDAY — APRIL 20.

BILL ODDIE is a remarkable person. Years ago he became well known as a comic actor. Now he has made many television appearances as an authority on bird life.

I liked one programme about migration in which he showed a swallow, newly arrived. "They say one swallow doesn't make a Summer," he commented. "That's right — it makes a miracle! This little chap has flown thousands of miles from Africa, through countless dangers and made it."

A reminder that Our Lord protects even his smallest creations.

WEDNESDAY — APRIL 21.

TWO little boys were visiting their grandfather when they saw his telescope on a shelf.

"Oh, look," cried Ben, picking it up, "it makes everything look much larger!"

Charlie took it and peered through the other end. "No it doesn't," he said indignantly. "It makes things smaller!"

Fortunately their grandfather was on hand to explain and to settle the dispute but nevertheless, that story did set me thinking. How often, I wonder, do quarrels spring up simply because those involved are convinced that only they have the correct way of looking at things?

Next time we feel like that, perhaps we should remember that very often another person's perspective can be just as valid as our own. That's my point of view, anyway!

A GUIDING HAND

THURSDAY— APRIL 22.

IN a way, life may be said to have some sort of connection with a greengrocer's shop:

In *currant* events, *raisin* optimistic notions is a *peach* of an idea. Being *sloe* to criticise others without justification is a *plum* prospect. Make a *date* with honest endeavour, that cares not a *fig* for futile practices. *Prune* prejudice, and upset the *apple*-cart of intolerance.

FRIDAY — APRIL 23.

I OFTEN feel that too much emphasis is put on the sad things in this still wonderful world. That's why I give full marks to The Society Of Happy People, based in the town of Irving, Texas.

Members have identified 21 types of happiness and want people to realise how diverse the experience of happiness can be. Among these are the joys of anticipation, fun, celebration, surprise, giving and contentment.

Isn't it good to know there are so many ways of finding happiness in life?

SATURDAY — APRIL 24.

JILL had been through a tough spell when things went badly wrong for her. But when I met her she was looking cheerful as she always did.

"It was something a friend said that got me through," she told me. "He used to live in Africa where he heard a proverb: 'When the storm passes over, the grasses will rise up again'."

SUNDAY — APRIL 25.

AND Jesus went about all Galilee, teaching in their synagogues, and preaching the gospel of the kingdom, and healing all manner of sickness and all manner of disease among the people.

Matthew 4:23

MONDAY — APRIL 26.

"THE man or woman who fears limits his activities." That was a maxim of Henry Ford who founded the great Ford manufacturing company and introduced motor cars to millions.

He was a person of great motivation, inspiring both himself and others. I like what he once said about the word failure:

"Failure is only the opportunity for a person to intelligently begin again."

A thought that has inspired so many to put defeat behind them and find success later.

TUESDAY — APRIL 27.

THESE simple words were chipped out on the wall of an underground cellar in Cologne, Germany, while a courageous group of Jewish men and women were hiding from the Nazis during the Second World War:

We believe in the sun even when it is not shining;
We believe in love even when we are not
feeling it;
We believe in God even when he is silent.

Lines to inspire us today, too.

SCENE AT
THE SHORE

WEDNESDAY — APRIL 28.

I REMEMBER many years ago a kind acquaintance talking about one of her friends.

"She's very nice," she told me. "We get on well, but she's very unreliable." At the time I found it difficult to understand how you could like someone you couldn't rely on.

However, through the years, I've tried to follow her example, and accept people as they are, faults and all! It hasn't been easy, but when I've started to say to myself: "The trouble with them . . ." I've learned to turn it around to say, "The trouble with me!"

Accepting others' faults can be difficult, but looking at our own is much harder. We can all try, though, and we may even make an improvement!

THURSDAY — APRIL 29.

I LIKE this Thought For Today: "Enjoy the little things of life. There may come a time when you realise they were the big things."

FRIDAY — APRIL 30.

EACH day is a present, perfect and new
Given by Heaven for me and for you,
Given to mould and to shape how we will
With words and behaviour, for good or for ill.
So let us, each morning, resolve on a plan
To use every moment as best as we can
And fill every hour in just such a way
To show the Lord thanks for His gift of this day.

Margaret Ingall.

May

SATURDAY— MAY 1.

SHARING LOVE

HAVE you a song within your heart,
Have you a smile to share?
Have you a moment in the day
To show someone you care?
Have you the time to be a friend
And listen when they call?
Have you the courage every day
To step out, walking tall?

Have you a hope for all mankind
Whatever faith or creed?
Have you the strength to show the way
To those who are in need?
If you've a song, a smile, a hope,
A special dream or two,
You have discovered love, my friend,
And love discovered you!

Iris Hesselden.

SUNDAY — MAY 2.

AND my people shall dwell in a peaceable habitation, and in sure dwellings, and in quiet resting places.

Isaiah 32:18

NATURE'S POWER

MONDAY — MAY 3.

WHEN a pair of blackbirds made their nest in a bush in the playground of a primary school in a rather deprived area of one of our large cities, the teachers shook their heads. It would never be left alone, they said.

But it was, thanks to Mr Abbot, the caretaker. "I showed it to the kids," he said, "and told them that each egg had a song inside it. If they wanted to hear the songs they would have to let them be."

It worked. The eggs hatched safely and the fledglings survived. Now every time the children hear a blackbird sing they remember the eggs they cared for.

TUESDAY — MAY 4.

MANY people visit Coniston, formerly the Lakeland home of John Ruskin. They explore the village church, the museum and go to Brantwood where Ruskin lived for the latter part of his life.

However, much as he loved the countryside and the Lake District he spent many months in the grim towns and cities of the industrial north, and farther afield. His main objective was to encourage ordinary people to use their God-given talents — even to discover their existence in the first place.

Ruskin firmly believed this adage: "In every person that comes near you, look for what is good and strong, honour that; rejoice in it, and as you can imitate it."

WEDNESDAY — MAY 5.

THERE'S a Lancashire saying which goes: "From clogs to clogs in three generations." This happened to a Liverpool merchant who failed in business through no fault of his own.

His clergyman called to sympathise and found him down in the dumps. "Everything has gone," he moaned. "I've lost everything."

"Oh, dear," came the reply, "so you've lost your reputation?"

"Indeed, I haven't, thank God!" came the quick reply. "My name and my reputation are fine!"

"Has your wife left you?"

"Indeed not. My wife is an angel — loyal, true and kind."

"I see," said the clergyman. "Now, your children — have they turned from you?"

"No, indeed," the merchant replied. "I never seemed to know my children until this happened, in fact. They've been so brave and sympathetic — I can't tell you how much they mean to me."

"Well," said his confidant, "you told me that you had lost everything but in fact you have lost nothing except a bag full of gold that doesn't really matter. Love, loyalty, comradeship — all the important things are still yours."

THURSDAY — MAY 6.

TRY to spend a couple of minutes thinking about these wise words today: "To forgive is to set a prisoner free and discover the prisoner was you."

FRIDAY — MAY 7.

THE Lady of the House was visiting a large store and had just stepped into the lift when a harassed-looking woman hurried in after her.

Examining the array of buttons for different floors, she gave a sigh. "Oh, I do wish that there was one marked 'next summer's holiday'. It would be so wonderful to find myself there right now."

Although, when later recounting the event, the Lady of the House and I shared some sympathetic laughter, I'm not sure that young woman had quite the right idea about life.

Not only is the desire to leap from one high spot to the next impractical, it's also rather wasteful. We can't expect to enjoy every single moment of our life, but I do think we should try to appreciate as many stops along the way as we can!

SATURDAY — MAY 8.

SOME years ago I read how a Welsh evangelist suggested this spiritual and physical exercise when one of his congregation complained that she felt God never seemed to answer her prayers.

He listened thoughtfully and then advised her, "Lift up your right arm with the fingers of the hand outstretched. Then close your fingers as if grasping an unseen hand above your head."

He explained that this action would illustrate the belief that she was putting her hand straight into the hand of God.

SUNDAY — MAY 9.

AND he leaping up stood, and walked, and entered with them into the temple, walking, and leaping, and praising God.

Acts 3:8

MONDAY — MAY 10.

THE writer Kenneth C. Steven has penned many thoughtful poems at his home in the beautiful Perthshire village of Dunkeld. I'd like to share this one — "Prayer" — with you:

Even though I only have
One window in my walls
And down below the gloom and grime
Of dark, forbidding halls —

Help me to see in that small square
Of sky you've given me,
The rainbow's water colour play,
And stars that blaze out free.

TUESDAY — MAY 11.

HOPE . . . where would we be without it? Samuel Johnson said that it was "the chief happiness which this world affords." Martin Luther said, "Everything that is done in the world is done by hope."

An old proverb calls it "the poor man's breakfast." There is truth in that for it costs nothing and keeps our spirits high on the darkest days.

Long, long live hope!

THE GREEN
GRASS OF HOME

WEDNESDAY — MAY 12.

THE Lady of the House and I had been watching a documentary about a stately home. It was a glorious building full of beautiful objects, but the thing which most impressed us was an interview with the proprietor.

Asked how he felt about possessing such a wonderful place, he revealed that he didn't regard himself as the owner, simply the current custodian. He felt privileged to enjoy the house and its contents, but knew that, like those who had gone before, his real job was looking after everything for future generations.

"It's a good philosophy for everyone," observed the Lady of the House. "We may not all live in stately homes, but we can still look after our own little corner. This world is such a beautiful inheritance — it's a shame not to give it a bit of polish before we hand it on!"

THURSDAY — MAY 13.

HERE are three thoughts on children to ponder today:

"Children have more need of models than critics." Joseph Joubert.

"Children have never been very good at listening to their elders, but they have never failed to imitate them." James Baldwin.

"Children need lots of love, especially when they don't deserve it!" Harold Hulbert.

FRIDAY — MAY 14.

TIME FACTORS

IF it's ten o'clock in Athens,
It's quite different in Tangier.
If it's noon in Casablanca,
Clocks don't show that in Kashmir.

Though languages will differ,
This point is paramount —
Let's translate it into English,
"Make every minute count."

John M. Robertson.

SATURDAY — MAY 15.

IT isn't easy to be poor, especially in a society where many equate worth with the ability to acquire wealth. People can find themselves being judged by what they look like on the outside, rather than what they're really like on the inside.

Hudson Taylor, the great missionary, was once asked with rather bemused admiration if it wasn't difficult to lead such a hand-to-mouth existence.

"Yes," he agreed. "But it's from God's hand to my mouth."

SUNDAY — MAY 16.

AND the parched ground shall become a pool, and the thirsty land springs of water.

Isaiah 35:7

MONDAY — MAY 17.

BETTY was rushing around the supermarket one afternoon, going up and down numerous aisles, reaching high and low as she gradually ticked off everything on her list.

Her trolley was almost full, but she still found a corner for a colourful pot plant. This'll cheer John up, she thought. I know he's been under pressure at work, although he doesn't say much.

Meanwhile, husband John was on his way home from work, and as he passed a florist's shop he thought, I'll buy some flowers for Betty — she's had an anxious time lately. Great-Aunt Nell has needed so much help, and our neighbour Ian is still in hospital.

Two loving minds with but one single thought. No wonder they laughed together so happily that evening as they arranged their combined floral display. And no wonder both felt renewed in spirit, able to tackle problems in good heart.

TUESDAY — MAY 18.

WE are all faced with some problem, new or old, from time to time. One afternoon when things were in a bit of a muddle, our friend Jennifer suggested that we take these words to heart:

"Try to remember that this life — yours and mine — is not a problem to solve, but a gift to cherish."

That way, she said, you will be able to stay one up on what used to get you down.

WEDNESDAY — MAY 19.

WHEN a group of refugees arrived in an English town a welcome gathering was laid on. As one woman spoke to the newcomers in their own tongue and others plied them with tea and scones, an elderly disabled woman said, "I'm so sorry. I can't do anything for them."

"Yes, you can," said one of the organisers. "You can smile."

It's often enough.

THURSDAY — MAY 20.

GRACE is the sort of person who always tries to look on the bright side of life. It's a trait I admire and one afternoon, after she had been regaling me with a humorous account of a fairly disastrous holiday, I told her so.

"Thank you, Francis," she said, "but it's really all due to Miss Cameron. You see, when I was a little girl many years ago, I went to a tiny village school. We had a wonderful teacher, but the school itself was very short of funds. When it came to art classes we had to make do with a poor collection of paints, but Miss Cameron always told us that even if we couldn't have the brightest colours, we could still do our best to paint happy pictures. And I've never forgotten the advice!"

I like the sound of Miss Cameron. Next time your own palette seems a bit muddy, remember her words.

FRIDAY — MAY 21.

I AM sure that there are times in everyone's life when the path ahead seems hard, but I do like these wise words from the pen of writer Victor Hugo:

"Have courage for the great sorrows of life and patience for the small ones, and when you have laboriously accomplished your daily task, go to sleep in peace. God is awake."

Now, don't you think that's a comforting thought?

SATURDAY — MAY 22.

OUR friend Sheila is easily hurt when someone utters an unkind word. She also dislikes gossip which puts a neighbour or an acquaintance in a bad light.

Many people tend to forget that words can hurt. But no one means all he or she says, and that's a fact of life worth remembering, too.

I think the best advice came from the lips of Mother Teresa when she said: "Kind words are short and easy to speak, but their echoes are truly endless."

How true! Words can be slippery things, wriggling out of our control, so handle them with care.

SUNDAY— MAY 23.

I THANK God through Jesus Christ our Lord.

Romans 7:25

MONDAY — MAY 24.

MAKE your home a happy home
A really well-loved place,
Where everyone is greeted
With a calm and cheerful face.
Smiles, kind words and gentleness,
A caring atmosphere,
The warmth of love, a helping hand
A look that is sincere.

Let it be a place of peace
Where people love to come,
And leave the burdens of the day
And drop them one by one.
Let all who come unto the door
Be comforted and blessed,
And leave to go their way again
Uplifted and refreshed.

Kathleen Gillum.

TUESDAY— MAY 25.

THANKS to countless films, radio shows and stage appearances, Bob Hope created a reputation as one of the world's greatest comics. At his 82nd birthday party, he told his guests:

"I think it's wonderful you could all be here for the forty-third anniversary of my thirty-ninth birthday. We decided not to light the candles this year — we were afraid Pan Am would mistake it for a runway."

It is good to be able to make a joke about advancing years — much better, surely, than letting the advancing years get you down.

WEDNESDAY — MAY 26.

A CHURCH group was discussing the Biblical story of Ruth and Naomi.

"It's like a novel," said one, "a love story."

"I think it is a very sad story," said another, "because in the beginning Naomi had lost all that was precious to her, her husband and her two sons and it made her bitter."

"Yes," continued the first speaker, "but look how happily it ended and that's what is important."

An old saying reminds us that we "get bitter — or get better." It makes me think of that great statesman Nelson Mandela who never allowed bitterness to gain a foothold. During his long imprisonment on Robben Island he wrote: "I knew people expected me to harbour anger . . . but I wanted South Africa to see that I loved my enemies."

Truly an example to challenge and inspire us.

THURSDAY — MAY 27.

DO you know this little prayer for reciting when we rise to a new day?

All praise to thee who safe has kept,
And hast refreshed me while I slept.
Guard my first springs of thought and will.
And with thyself my spirit fill.

Composed by a person unknown, this is a blend of borrowed lines from the hymn "All praise to thee who safe has kept", written by Thomas Ken, who was born in 1637.

FLORAL TRIBUTE

FRIDAY — MAY 28.

A CORRESPONDENT has sent me this "Gardener's Prayer", found in a New Zealand paper:

"Lord, grant that in some way it may rain every day, say from about midnight until three o'clock in the morning, but you see, it must be gentle and warm so that it can soak in. Grant at the same time that it should not rain on the campion, alyssum, helianthemum, lavender and the others which You in your wisdom know are drought-loving plants — I will write the names on a bit of paper if you like.

"And grant that the sun may shine the whole day through but not everywhere (for instance, not on spiraea, gentian or rhododendron) and not too much. That there may be plenty of dew and very little wind, enough worms, no mealy bugs, slugs or snails, no mildew or fungus, and that once a week thin liquid manure may fall from the heavens — Amen."

Gardeners don't ask for much, do they . . ?

SATURDAY — MAY 29.

THE thoughtful proverbs of the Chinese people are world famous. Here is one to reflect on today:

"When I dig another person out of trouble, the hole from which I lift him is the place where I bury my own."

Try it — helping your neighbour with his problems helps us to solve our own.

SUNDAY — MAY 30.

BELOVED, let us love one another: for love is of God; and every one that loveth is born of God, and knoweth God.

John 1st Epistle: 4:7

MONDAY — MAY 31.

THE Lady of the House and I often spend a happy hour or two indulging in one of our favourite occupations — browsing round a well-stocked second-hand bookshop. Apart from the treasures on the shelves, we find the combination of mustiness and quietness quite irresistible.

Here are to be found what Charles Lamb perhaps had in mind when he spoke of "books of the true sort", while the poet John Milton's comment was: "A good book is the precious life-blood of a master spirit, enbalmed and treasured upon purpose to a life beyond life."

In Elizabeth Goudge's novel "A City Of Bells", Jocelyn Irvin's bookshop near the cathedral features prominently, as do an elderly clergyman and his two young grandsons. On one of their regular visits to the bookshop, Grandfather remarks:

"It is the most friendly vocation in the world. A bookseller is the link between mind and mind, the feeder of the hungry, very often the binder up of wounds. Yes . . . it's a great vocation . . . booksellers are the salt of the earth."

It's a philosophy with which I heartily agree!

June

TUESDAY — JUNE 1.

WHAT is it that we all seek but often don't know we've found until afterwards?

The answer? Happiness. For it's true, isn't it? It's not till we look back, sometimes long afterwards, that we realise how happy we were.

So the secret of happiness is realising that we have it now and living every day thankful for our good fortune.

WEDNESDAY — JUNE 2.

WHEN Eric first qualified as a teacher he had high ideals, but soon found his working life could be challenging.

"Most of my pupils were eager to leave and find jobs," he told me. "They felt they'd had enough of learning, and the harder I tried to teach them, the less I succeeded. Then I came across some very sensible words by a Victorian writer called Sir Arthur Helps. He said:

'Wise sayings often fall on barren ground, but a kind word is never thrown away.' "

Eric smiled. "So next time I felt disheartened, instead of scolding, I offered encouragement. What a difference it made — not only to their attitude, but to mine. By the time they left, we had all learned something of value."

THURSDAY — JUNE 3.

BREATHING SPACE

SOMETIMES all that's needed is
A little breathing space,
Time to stop and do things at
A slightly slower pace.

We tend to rush on through the day
Just trying to fit things in,
Using up the energy
Of nerves and mind and limb.

Life was never meant to be
All tear and rush and race —
So why not ease the reins a bit
And make a breathing space?

Kathleen Gillum.

FRIDAY — JUNE 4.

A FRIEND'S eyes lit up with pleasure when he saw these two notices, which were pinned up side by side, in the middle of a big city office one day:

I am the master of what I keep to myself and the slave of what I say.

I will reap what I plant; if I plant gossip I will harvest suspicion, if I plant love I will harvest happiness.

He wasn't surprised to learn that he had visited one of the most successful workplaces in town. The smiling faces of the staff told him so, too.

SATURDAY — JUNE 5.

WHEN Julie twisted her ankle just before she was due to begin her annual leave, it seemed like a disaster. "But the funny thing is," she told me, "that once I'd accepted that I wouldn't be going away, it actually turned into one of the nicest holidays I've ever had.

"I read books, I sketched and painted and, when the weather was sunny, I just sat in the garden and enjoyed all the plants and flowers and the birdsong that I never usually have time to notice. In fact, when I went back to work I was far more relaxed and rested than I ever normally am!"

Doesn't it just go to show that a positive attitude can turn a piece of bad luck into a bonus?

SUNDAY — JUNE 6.

AND the word of God increased; and the number of the disciples multiplied in Jerusalem greatly.

Acts 6:7

MONDAY — JUNE 7.

SEVENTY years young.
Not seventy years old!
Remember, new joys
Are about to unfold!
Seventy years show
Your new age of grace,
Not the wrinkles of life —
But the smile on your face!

Elizabeth Gozney.

TUESDAY — JUNE 8.

THERE'S a story about two men in a hospital ward. One was able to sit up for a short time and look out of the window, while the other had to lie flat on his back.

Every afternoon the man by the window would look outside and describe everything he could see — the park with the lake where there were ducks and swans; the children feeding the ducks and sailing their boats; the stretches of grass and flower beds, and in the distance a bowling green. His descriptions made his friend feel that he could almost see what was happening outside.

One day, the man by the window went home and the other man asked if he could be moved to the coveted place by the window. With difficulty, he stretched his head to view the lovely scene. He was looking out on to the car park.

As it has truly been said, life is what we make it.

WEDNESDAY — JUNE 9.

A FRIEND saw this piece of advice on the notice board of a church in the heart of New York: "You are not fully dressed until you put a smile on."

He soon realised the immediate impact that the words had made. For the next half-hour, as he went on his way through the crowded city streets, every second person was smiling back at his happy face.

"I had got the message," he said. "And dozens of strangers were now getting it through me!"

THURSDAY — JUNE 10.

YOUNG Laura is quite a philosopher in her own way and she was wondering one day what it would be like to meet the perfect man. "It might even be a let-down," she mused. "The perfect man might prove to be surprisingly boring!"

We were discussing an article she had read in which the writer, Frederick Forsyth, had given a description of an ideal man. He should show "strength without brutality, honesty without priggishness, courage without recklessness, humour without frivolity, humanity without sentimentality, intelligence without deviousness, scepticism without cynicism."

"A wonderful description," I commented, "but apart from one man who lived more than 2000 years ago, impossible to attain."

"Ah, yes, Francis," came the reply, "yet there's nothing to stop us from *trying* to attain it — it's a great example to follow." How true; we should never stop trying to do our best.

FRIDAY — JUNE 11.

WHEN all the world seems sad and grey
And man-to-man unkind,
It's in the hand of friendship
True beauty that you'll find.
With loving thoughts and kindly deeds
They'll many a doubt dispel
Dark shadows flee from out your mind —
And suddenly, all is well!

Jenny Chaplin.

FULL STEAM AHEAD

SATURDAY — JUNE 12.

HOW often do we hear people say that they love the dawn hour when the sun peeps up in the sky?

We each have our favourite time of day. Some folk love late afternoon when their family are coming home from work and school, while others go for the reflective time before midnight when the accumulated thoughts of the day are with us. Late-bedders like to sit and think in "the wee small hours."

We are, each and all, different in our choices. Take the hour you like best — and, with friends or just alone, enjoy it . . .

SUNDAY — JUNE 13.

BUT God commendeth his love towards us, in that, while we were yet sinners, Christ died for us.

Romans 5:8

MONDAY — JUNE 14.

LONG memories are excellent if recollections are positive, not the unhappy kind.

Winifred Holtby, the famous Yorkshire novelist, had an admirable attitude towards life. She once observed that she tried to follow the viewpoint of the former statesman, Lord Balfour. He had affirmed, "I'm quite unable to harbour resentment for long because I always forget the reason why I was originally angry."

Now that's a quote that *is* worth remembering.

TUESDAY — JUNE 15.

SOME friends have three sweet little daughters, as beautiful as if they had just walked out of a fairy tale. They love their grandparents very much and like nothing more than going to their house to visit. One day, they were bitterly disappointed because there seemed no time whatsoever during that week when their beloved grandparents had a free day.

"Can we come tomorrow?" the first asked with big eyes.

"I'm afraid not," was the answer.

"Could we come today?" the next pleaded. There had to be a sad shaking of the head to this suggestion, too. Finally the third had an idea.

"Could we come yesterday then?"

WEDNESDAY — JUNE 16.

I FOUND this little verse in a Chatterbox Annual (1914), a timely incentive to do things sooner rather than later:

Don't talk about things you are going to do,
Don't say that you mean to be noble and true,
Don't wait till tomorrow to make up your mind
That you'll make others happy, and always
be kind;
For tomorrow you'll talk as you're talking today,
And your good resolutions will vanish away.
Do it now — let the world see you mean to
be true!
Oh! Don't talk of the things you are going to do!

THURSDAY — JUNE 17.

I'D like to share this thought-provoking poem with you today. Think about the images behind each verse and I hope you will be inspired to make your own contribution to the lives of those around you:

INSPIRATION

One smile begins a friendship
One handclasp lifts a soul,
One star can guide a ship at sea
One word can frame the goal.

One step must start each journey
One word must start each prayer,
One hope will raise our spirits
One touch can show you care.

One voice can speak with wisdom
One heart can know what's true,
One life can make a difference —
You see, it's up to you!

Olive Beazley-Long.

FRIDAY— JUNE 18.

HAVE you lots of fresh food in your fridge and dozens of tins in your larder? I expect so.

We all tend to take these things for granted, and yet there are millions of not-so-fortunate people in the world for whom they will always be only a dream.

Think of them today.

SATURDAY — JUNE 19.

SEVERAL days of heavy rain had made the weather the main topic of conversation, but the Lady of the House and I had to smile when she quoted a poem she had been taught as a child:

A daily dose of sunshine
Is never guaranteed
However much we'd like it,
However much in need.
But if you save some sunshine
And tuck it in your smile
You'll find a little sunny spell
Can last for quite a while.

I might try that as soon as it stops raining!

SUNDAY — JUNE 20.

AND I will deliver thee out of the hand of the wicked, and I will redeem thee out of the hand of the terrible. Jeremiah 15:21

MONDAY — JUNE 21.

A NEIGHBOUR who was moving house asked me if I would accept several old notebooks which he had prized for four decades. In one, I came on these words by a 19th-century writer and biologist, Thomas Henry Huxley, who died in 1895:

"The rung of a ladder was never meant to rest upon, but only to support you long enough to enable you to reach for something higher."

A thought worth keeping in mind.

TUESDAY — JUNE 22.

A NEIGHBOUR had a "crash" on his home computer, and lost much of the data which he had filed. Valuable information, such as addresses of friends and relations and personal files, had all gone after two years of industrious and steady compiling.

A rather nasty electronic virus, it was found, had penetrated via e-mail.

"It was just one of those things," he said. "Computers are wonderful but they are as temperamental as their owners."

I had to admire Michael's calm reaction and his response to a difficult situation. Now, isn't there a lesson here for all of us, including those without a computer?

Accidents and minor mishaps will happen, and we have to face up to them in a reasonable and constructive way. As an old adage, familiar to countless generations, puts it, there's no use getting angry "over spilled milk".

WEDNESDAY — JUNE 23.

THUMBING through an old magazine I came on this quotation which I'd like to share with you today. Exactly who first said it is not known, but I feel that the thought is worth keeping in mind:

"A man's character and his garden both reflect the amount of weeding that was done during the growing season."

THURSDAY — JUNE 24.

ARE you the kind of person who tends to take on too much? I regularly come across friends like that.

Many a mother falls into this category, doing more than her fair share of jobs about the house. Whenever I meet people like this — the "over-workers" I call them — I recall an old Turkish proverb:

"The wise man remembers that two water melons cannot be held under one arm."

FRIDAY — JUNE 25.

SYLVIA had always been a worrier. Often she would lie awake at night, brooding over the day's events and fretting about problems that hadn't even arisen. Then one day her young niece gave her a present she had made at school. It was a piece of cross-stitch, carefully worked with the maxim "Count Your Blessings".

"I was so pleased with it," Sylvia told me, "that I hung it up at once. But it wasn't until that night, when I was tossing and turning as usual that I thought about the words Sarah had stitched.

"Right there and then I resolved that every time a problem popped into my head, I would deliberately try thinking of a blessing instead. And do you know, it works! The only trouble is there are so many blessings, that I'm afraid some of them get left out altogether . . ."

Sylvia hasn't totally got over her worrying, but she's definitely getting better!

HOUSE AND GARDEN

SATURDAY — JUNE 26.

MURIEL had always dreamed of travelling the world, but she had to wait for years until it was possible for her to embark on a long-anticipated touring holiday abroad. Neighbours and friends received rapt postcards and promises that when she returned she would tell them more about the wonderful things she had seen.

"All the same," Muriel confided to me later, "I wasn't looking forward to getting back until I actually arrived, and then I found that my friends had arranged a surprise party for me, serving food from all the places I had visited. They brought pasta, pizza, olives, goat's cheese, vine leaves, honey cakes and everything else you could think of! It was such fun and it really made me appreciate being home again."

"It sounds wonderful!" I laughed.

"Ah, but the very best part of all," she smiled, "was discovering that my friends really do think the world of me!"

SUNDAY — JUNE 27.

HE that is joined unto the Lord is one spirit.

Corinthians I 6:17

MONDAY — JUNE 28.

WISE words for you to reflect on today from an old proverb:

Patience is power; with time and patience the mulberry leaf becomes silk.

TUESDAY — JUNE 29.

IN the years before he died in April 2001, Jimmy Logan, the well-known entertainer and actor, was asked on many occasions to speak a few suitable words at the funerals of friends and fellow-performers.

Being a man whose profession was to entertain others, he believed very much in the value of laughter in life. Here, in his own words, is how, closing his eulogy, he felt a person should be remembered:

Remember me by the laughter, not the tears,
Remember me for the joy and fun we shared
Through all the happy years,
Please think of me, if you will, with a smile
When we all shared jokes, and laughed
At things we did a wee bit daft.

So, if you smile, and if you laugh,
Sing songs, share fun and joy,
Then I will join you in the toast,
And if you want to think of me,
Lift up your glass so I can share;
Enjoy yourselves
And I'll be there.

WEDNESDAY — JUNE 30.

AT cool of day, with God I walk
My garden's grateful shade;
I hear His voice among the trees
And I am not afraid.

Anon.

July

THURSDAY — JULY 1.

SOMETIMES, in the magic hush
Of a Summer morning,
When it's very, very early,
And all is calm and still,
When the dew shines bright as diamonds
On petals newly opened,
And the sun, on rosy-golden wings,
Illuminates the hill.

It only lasts a little while,
But there's a sense of wonder,
A gentle peace that comes before
The clamour of the day,
And in those precious moments,
In the quiet of the garden,
Something very beautiful
Seems but a step away.

Kathleen O'Farrell.

FRIDAY — JULY 2.

ALTHOUGH the English language is, on occasion, regarded as slightly baffling, there's nothing strange about the fact that in the school of life, it's wise to remember that understanding starts with "U".

SATURDAY — JULY 3.

IMPOSSIBLE DREAM

IF we never had to worry,
And never had a care;
If everybody in the world
Could be a millionaire;
If everything was perfect,
And life was like a song,
We'd likely look around and think
There must be something wrong.

John M. Robertson.

SUNDAY — JULY 4.

AND this I pray, that your love may abound yet more and more in knowledge and all judgement.

Philippians 1:9

MONDAY — JULY 5.

THERE are many wonderful signs of peace and mutual understanding in the world today. One of them is the way in which people of different religious traditions and beliefs find strength in each other's writings and prayers.

This prayer by Abu Bekr is shared by people of different faiths: "I thank you, Lord, for knowing me better than I know myself, and for letting me know myself better than others know me.

"Make me, I pray You, better than they suppose, and forgive me for what they do not know."

We can all say "Amen" to that!

TUESDAY — JULY 6.

SHOPPING today is a far cry from the grocers' shops of days gone by. One of the biggest differences which we notice is in the way things are packaged.

In the queue at the delicatessen counter one day, I couldn't help thinking that things had perhaps gone a little too far when I saw the sign on the daily special: "nanny goat cheese".

"Well," said a fellow customer, "how many of us have ever had billy goat cheese?"

Still, as I enjoyed the laugh along with my fellow shoppers, I realised that some things don't change whatever the packaging; queueing is less of a chore if you use the time to share a light-hearted moment.

WEDNESDAY — JULY 7.

THE fastest way of sending messages between people these days is via e-mail. Written on the computer screen by the sender, a message will appear on another screen in, say, Melbourne, Tokyo or Paris at just the click of a button.

In a similar kind of way I like to send what I call "H-mails" to people I care about. "Head"-mails are thoughts of love which I want to carry to those I know are in need for one reason or another.

A friend might be far from home; a relative might be ill or suffering loneliness. "H-mails" don't need electronic wizardry; they only need a loving heart.

THURSDAY — JULY 8.

HERE is a quotation which is a particular favourite of mine: "A faithful friend is the medicine of life."

Not long ago, the Lady of the House and I had cause to remember it once more. Isobel, a friend of ours, moved to another part of the country and we were unable to see her as often as we would have liked. We knew that she had many problems, but over the years, had become independent and learned how to cope.

Then we heard that she was not very well and we wrote to say how sorry we were, and how we regretted not being near enough to make regular visits. Isobel's reply, however, made us proud.

She said she knew that we had sent loving thoughts and good wishes, and they had been a source of great comfort. Her letter ended with the words: "You are always with me, the best friends anyone could have. I shall remember you always and be grateful."

If you, too, have a faithful friend, tell them now how much they mean to you.

FRIDAY — JULY 9.

IT had been a noisy meeting and angry words had been spoken. It looked like there would be no agreement until an elderly man stood up and in a quiet voice said, "Let's start again, and this time, let's all row the boat, not rock it."

Do you know, that meeting ended up one of the most successful I have ever attended!

SATURDAY — JULY 10.

THAT grand old man of letters, J. B. Priestley, when one month short of reaching 90 years old, said in a television interview shortly before his death:

"We live by admiration, hope and love . . . especially love."

Words of wisdom from a giant of literature and well worth taking to heart, don't you agree?

SUNDAY — JULY 11.

NOW the Lord of peace himself give you peace always by all means. The Lord be with you all.

Thessalonians II 3:16

MONDAY — JULY 12.

THESE words come from an old Birthday Book:

Sunshine in the morning, moonlight at night,
The fragrance of gardens, the deep silence of the forest,
The musical rattle of tea cups, the laughter of happy children,
The familiar tread of loved and approaching feet,
A beautiful thought, a pleasant dream, a letter of kindly greeting,
A worthwhile job to do, a joke, a song, a kindness received . . .
These are the things which cost us nothing, but enrich us beyond all telling.

I agree — and hope you will, too!

TUESDAY — JULY 13.

OUR language has changed so much in recent years — many new words are now included in our vocabulary. Words such as Internet and cyber-space are, for example, well known among the computer-conscious.

Another phrase that's being used more and more is "renewable commodity". Yet no matter what the linguistic modernists may say, "happiness" has been a "renewable commodity" for centuries — and you don't need to be a fully qualified scientist to prove it!

WEDNESDAY — JULY 14.

A NEIGHBOUR'S young nieces are given huge amounts of presents for Christmas, birthdays and many other special days in the calendar year. In fact, it has reached the stage where the family could almost, it has been jokingly suggested by some friends and relatives, invest in a second house just to contain all their daughters' gifts!

Despite the many dolls which the elder of the two receives — which talk and laugh, and even walk — her favourite is an ancient, battered doll that was nothing more than a hand-me-down. But that's the doll Ann loves.

Children teach us that despite our sometimes materialistic attitudes as adults, their standards are completely different. When they love, they love unconditionally.

BONNIE
BANKS

THURSDAY — JULY 15.

I LIKE this story of how the kettle found the perfect recipe for getting on in life. "Tell me how," she'd asked her friends in the kitchen.

"Take panes," said the window.
"Never be led," said the pencil.
"Do a driving business," said the hammer.
"Aspire to great things," said the nutmeg grater.
"Make light of everything," said the fire.
"Make much of small things," said the pair of spectacles.
"Never do anything offhand," said the glove.
"Just reflect," said the mirror.
"Be sharp," said the knife.
"Find a good thing and stick to it," said the glue.

And that's why in almost every kitchen in the land, the kettle sings so happily as she works. I'm sure there's a lesson here for us all.

FRIDAY — JULY 16.

ONE of our local churches holds its own "Songs Of Praise" service every few months after the congregation has voted for their favourite hymns. "How Great Thou Art" is always at or near the top of the list.

One month the congregation was told, "You, too, can be great. Some people are great because for them no task is too big, but true greatness is often found in those for whom no task is too small to be worthy of their time and effort, so let us care for each other in all the small ways we can, then we will achieve greatness."

SATURDAY — JULY 17.

A FRIEND who admits she has made her fair share of mistakes sent me this little collection of thoughts on what people have said about making them:

"A life spent in making mistakes is not only more honourable but more useful than a life spent in doing nothing." George Bernard Shaw.

"A mistake is a lesson on its way to being learned." Anon.

"Mistakes are the portals of discovery."
James Joyce.

"Instruction does not prevent the making of mistakes; and mistakes themselves are often the best teachers of all."
James A. Froude, English historian.

SUNDAY — JULY 18.

AS for me, I will call upon God; and the Lord shall save me. Psalms 55:16

MONDAY — JULY 19.

ARRIVING home one evening I was admiring a bank of colour at the roadside. Even when I realised that the flowers were only dandelions, the carpet of yellow still looked lovely. After all "a weed is just a flower in the wrong place."

It struck me that the same principle can apply to people. Sometimes they feel ill at ease where they are, like a plant in soil that doesn't suit it, but look deep inside and you'll see beauty blossoming.

TUESDAY — JULY 20.

OUR friend Audrey has great enthusiasm for brightening up her daily routine and derives enormous satisfaction from both work and leisure.

She told us recently: "Can you imagine a world where nobody gets enthusiastic or excited about what they are doing?"

The American writer Og Mandino, who inspired so many of his readers, once said: "Every memorable act in the history of the world has been a triumph of enthusiasm. Nothing great is ever achieved without it because it gives any challenge or any occupation, no matter how frightening or difficult, a new meaning.

"Without enthusiasm you are doomed to a life of mediocrity, but with it you can accomplish miracles."

WEDNESDAY — JULY 21.

WHEN Fred told me he and Lisa were to be married you could have knocked me down with a feather.

"But I thought you couldn't stand each other!" I said.

"That was when we first met."

So often this happens. It can take time to get to know people and, you know, first impressions are frequently wrong. A very wise English writer, Frank Swinnerton, once said, "Nine out of ten people improve on acquaintance."

I know Fred and Lisa would agree!

THURSDAY — JULY 22.

A PRAYER AT BEDTIME

I BRING you my mistakes, Lord,
The failures of today,
I hope You will forgive them
And sweep them all away.

So many things I should have said,
The things I've left undone,
The battles I avoided,
And those I should have won.

Then when tomorrow comes, Lord,
A day unspoilt and new,
With all my failures left behind,
I'll start afresh with You.

Iris Hesselden.

FRIDAY — JULY 23.

IN Arctic Norway, in the middle of Summer, some people hardly go to bed at all. The sun is up both day and night and it isn't unusual to hear people mowing their lawns at three in the morning!

Everyone you meet is excited; they are celebrating the return of the light after enduring several months of near total darkness.

To witness this is a reminder of how we should constantly give thanks for the abundance of wonderful gifts He has showered upon us.

SATURDAY — JULY 24.

MANY readers may remember the novels of the well-known Methodist preacher and author, William Riley. They might even recall their grandparents being devotees of his work.

Some of these novels may seem rather old-fashioned these days but one, "A Village In Craven", paints a picture of more settled times. It describes the village personalities including the cobbler, Dicky Isherwood.

When hearing of anyone's troubles he always reminded customers in his shop that they could give help and what he called "A Lift On The Way". He was never afraid to quote the words: "I will trust and not be afraid."

Surely this is a message just as applicable today.

SUNDAY — JULY 25.

AND the peace of God, which passeth all understanding shall keep your hearts and minds through Christ Jesus.

Philippians 4:7

MONDAY — JULY 26.

HERE are some "Thoughts For The Day" which you might like to share:

We need the power of love, not the love of power.

Let us make silver linings with other people's clouds.

People need love especially when they don't deserve it.

TUESDAY — JULY 27.

JOURNEYS! What an exciting word. Even the sound conjures up pictures of faraway exotic places. It's surely a word to stir the imagination and fuel flights of fancy. Where might these journeys take us? To the wonders of the East? The beauty of the South Seas? The wide open spaces — and cities — of the United States and Canada?

Now, do you know the most wonderful thing of all? We need never leave the comfort of home and our own armchair. Thanks to colourful travel books and television programmes, the whole world is at our feet. Whether made by boat, train or plane — or simply in our imagination — journeys are a wonderful experience!

Enjoy them all.

WEDNESDAY — JULY 28.

SUMMER KEEPSAKE

THE sun on my shoulders,
The sand 'neath my toes,
The dancing sea breezes
That tickle my nose,
The taste of the ocean
Leaves salt on my lips,
The cry of the seagull
That hovers and dips.
These gifts of the Summer,
So bright and so clear
Will warm and sustain me
As Winter draws near.

Margaret Ingall.

THURSDAY — JULY 29.

A RATHER daring gentleman of our acquaintance was brave enough to intervene in a heated exchange between an irate mother and her teenage daughter. And the final words of wisdom he left with them were these:

"Always remember two important things . . . all we have is each other. And the only moment in time which is ours is now."

How true!

FRIDAY — JULY 30.

THERE is an old American Indian greeting which goes:

"My heart is open, but my hand is empty."

This is simply a rather poetic way of saying that since the stranger carries no weapon, he comes in peace. A sentiment to cherish, surely.

SATURDAY — JULY 31.

YEARS ago milkmen came round with their cans and half-pint or one-pint measures. The milk was poured into a jug or basin and our family always knew when our milkman was near, even without seeing his milkfloat. Through the air would come the sound of his cheerful whistling.

Our neighbour who lived alone maintained that he helped to cheer the start of her day with his whistling and happy face. Now, we may not go around whistling but we can certainly cultivate a cheerful face and responsive attitude to others.

August

SUNDAY — AUGUST 1.

THE grace of the Lord Jesus Christ, and the love of God, and the communion of the Holy Ghost, be with you all. Amen. Corinthians II 13:14

MONDAY — AUGUST 2.

ANGELS

WHEN the road is steep and rocky
And the way is hard to find,
When your problems all oppress you
And the world seems so unkind,
Just reach out a hand in silence,
Take a moment you can spare,
Soon you'll feel your special angels
All around you everywhere.

When the night is dark and stormy
And the stars forget to shine,
When you feel that sleep eludes you
They will bring a peace divine.
When you see the sun awaken
And you sense a bright, new start,
You will know your special angels
Took your hand and touched your heart.

Iris Hesselden.

TUESDAY— AUGUST 3.

MISS WINTON was moving to a smaller house. I thought she would be heartbroken about having to dispose of so many of her possessions, but not a bit of it.

"There were so many things I haven't used or even looked at for years," she told me. "Now other people can enjoy them, give them a new lease of life."

The move has done the same for Miss Winton.

WEDNESDAY — AUGUST 4.

THE story of John Calvin Coolidge proves how true it is that hard work brings rewards. This farmer's son from Vermont studied long and hard, achieved distinction as a lawyer and was elected into office, in 1923, as President of the United States. Coolidge lived by these words:

Press on: nothing in the world can take the place of perseverance.
Talent will not; nothing is more common than unsuccessful men with talent.
Genius will not; unrewarded genius is almost a proverb.
Education will not; the world is full of educated derelicts.
Persistence and determination alone are omnipotent.

These are words we should all remember when we feel that we need that spark of genius. Disraeli, another statesman, put it: "The secret of success is consistency of purpose."

THURSDAY — AUGUST 5.

"DON'T you think there's a great deal we can learn from the story of Noah's Ark?" Molly said one day. Then she explained: "It's got all the things you need to help us make the most of life":

One: Don't miss the boat!

Two : Plan ahead. It wasn't raining when Noah built the vessel.

Three: Remember that we are all in the same boat.

FRIDAY — AUGUST 6.

COLIN'S garden is not very large and yet it's one which contains not only plants, but also a modest collection of unusual stones, colourful shells, and pieces of driftwood, all accumulated during his travels.

"Most of them," he told me, "are souvenirs of places I've visited, but the driftwood, in particular, has a special significance for me. You see, as a young man, I sometimes felt myself to be like a piece of flotsam, drifting and purposeless.

"I was beginning to lose all belief in the world until one day it occurred to me that sooner or later even a piece of driftwood will end up safely ashore — and usually moulded into an even more interesting shape because of its travels. It may sound odd, but from that moment on, I felt as if my faith in the future would be justified."

Isn't it wonderful how even the most humble of objects can play its part in inspiring trust in ourselves and our Creator?

SATURDAY — AUGUST 7.

HAS it ever struck you that so many of the healthiest and happiest people you meet are also the ones who laugh the most? I think Danny Kaye, the American comedian, summed it up when he said: "I feel I am making people happy just by coaxing them to laugh. When you make people laugh, you are really giving them the best medicine in the world."

Just what the doctor ordered, really. In fact Danny, all his life, nursed a burning ambition to be a doctor or surgeon, but I'm sure he did the next best thing by deciding to dispense laughter instead.

SUNDAY — AUGUST 8.

UNTO him be glory in the church by Christ Jesus throughout all ages, world without end. Amen.

Ephesians 3:21

MONDAY — AUGUST 9.

ALEX was a chemist before he retired. "You know, Francis," he said one day, "a chemical element can exist in different forms. I still find it amazing that carbon occurs as a diamond, a very hard substance, and also as graphite, the soft stuff sometimes known as black lead."

Now, doesn't that remind you of character? The hardest one can often betray a soft spot and, as for the so-called "soft people", they often display real backbone when faced with life's difficulties.

TUESDAY — AUGUST 10.

I'VE been reading about American artist Howard Chandler Christy. Born in 1873 in rural Ohio, his life contained its share of ups and downs, yet he still managed to rise to become one of his country's most celebrated sons, and a painter of many luminaries of his time, including President Roosevelt.

One remark of his stuck firmly in my mind: "Every morning," he said, "I spend fifteen minutes filling my mind full of God; and so there's no room left for worry."

I can't help thinking that such a habit must certainly have added inspiration to his brushstrokes!

WEDNESDAY — AUGUST 11.

AMONGST many book treasures is a small collection of poems "Forward To Victory" by Brigadier-Major S. Bramley-Moore, M.C., a well-known inventor.

Published in 1941 he explained: "The poems were the result of active experiences in the battle of life. They were written in the spirit of the moment or after some emergency."

One poem "In Time Of Trouble" was the outcome of financial and technical problems. Yet the final verse reminds us of God's faithfulness:

What'er befalls, what'er betides,
The Lord will be Thy constant Guide,
Rejoice and Praise
God's glorious ways.

Surely a message worth remembering.

THURSDAY — AUGUST 12.

I WAS delighted when a local clergyman, instead of a Biblical text, chose a single word as the subject of a sermon. The word in question was "decision" and he proved what can be done with just one word.

We all, of course, make many decisions in the course of a day and indeed we had all made a decision that morning to go to church! It reminded all of us of a decision made years ago to become committed Christians, and also reminded us that two thousand years ago three fishermen called Peter, James and John made a decision to follow Our Lord and become "Fishers Of Men".

Simple men, but what great impact their decision was to have on all of us.

FRIDAY — AUGUST 13.

THE German poet and philosopher Johann Wolfgang von Goethe, born in 1749, lived more than two centuries before television, computers and the Internet, but I don't think he wrote truer words than these:

"The world is so empty if one thinks only of mountains, rivers and cities; but to know someone here and there who thinks and feels with us, and though distant, is close to us in spirit — this makes the earth for us an inhabited garden."

May I suggest that, before today is over, you contact someone you know in a distant place to say a cheerful hello?

SATURDAY — AUGUST 14.

A FRIEND'S church magazine contains a section of items which have appeared in church bulletins, or were announced at church services. These humorous gems caught his eye and I hope that they will make you smile, too:

Miss Charlene Manson sang "I will not pass this way again," giving obvious pleasure to the congregation.

The eighth-graders will be presenting Shakespeare's Hamlet in the church at 7.00 p.m. The congregation are invited along to attend this tragedy.

SUNDAY — AUGUST 15.

THE Lord Jesus Christ be with thy spirit. Grace be with you. Amen. Timothy II 4:22

MONDAY — AUGUST 16.

FOR FUTURE REFERENCE

ON looking back, we tend to track
Mixed thoughts about the past.
Some are cheery, some are dreary.
Some fade, while others last.

Though history can guarantee
Its darker days, let's light
The Lamp of Hope, that gives us scope
To keep the future bright.

John M. Robertson.

IDEAL
HOME

TUESDAY — AUGUST 17.

DESPITE her busy job at a local health centre, Beryl's garden always looks good, so when I saw her weeding the flower beds one day, I took the chance to compliment her on her efforts.

"Ah, but I never think of gardening as a chore," she smiled. "In fact, I find there's something very soothing about it. Knowing that other hands have tended this land in the past and, hopefully, will do so long into the future, makes me feel that I'm part of a pattern, linked to a reality much greater than just my own little time and space. It helps to put all my trivial day-to-day problems into perspective."

WEDNESDAY — AUGUST 18.

HERE are some thoughts to remind us that moments of fear need not be as life-shattering as we often imagine:

"Fear is that little darkroom where negatives are developed."
Michael Pritchard.

"When you face your fear, most of the time you will discover that it was not really such a big threat after all. We all need some form of deeply rooted, powerful motivation — it empowers us to overcome obstacles so we can live our dreams."
Les Brown.

"Never fear shadows. They simply mean there's a light shining somewhere nearby."
Ruth E. Renkel.

THURSDAY — AUGUST 19.

AS children, twins Sarah and Steven were very different in temperament. Although both were clever, Sarah would frequently fret about her schoolwork, worrying if her marks were not quite as good as those of her friends. Steven, on the other hand, took a far more casual approach, and would often break the news of any indifferent results by telling his parents that at least he had done better than William or Jamie.

One day their mother taught them this rhyme:

Don't stare at other people, if the truth you
would be shown,
Don't examine their performance to compare
it with your own,
We each have a potential which is ours and
ours alone,
So measure by your own rule — then you'll
know if you have grown!

I know that rhyme helped Sarah and Steven — and I suspect it could help a great many of us!

FRIDAY — AUGUST 20.

OUR friend Evelyn is a person with a happy nature, quick to laugh and ready, in moments of stress, to help clear up a difficult situation. "The longer you carry a problem, the heavier it gets," she says.

We try to follow Evelyn's advice not to "take things too seriously." As she says, "live a life of serenity, not one of continuing regrets."

Good advice, don't you agree?

QUIET
REFLECTION

SATURDAY — AUGUST 21.

THE lines below were inside a small Victorian wooden box bought at a jumble sale and given by a mother to her young daughter:

I wish kind friends to love thee,
And wise ones thee to guide,
With happy ones to cheer thee,
Whatever may betide.

Isn't it a lovely message to pass on from one generation to the next?

SUNDAY — AUGUST 22.

FOR the grace of God that bringeth salvation hath appeared to all men.
Titus 2:11

MONDAY — AUGUST 23.

I LIKE this story which I heard about the couple who had celebrated their Golden Wedding anniversary. Somebody asked the lady of that house what was the secret of their long and happy marriage.

She replied, "Before our wedding day I decided to make a list of ten of my husband's faults which, for the sake of our marriage, I would always overlook."

"And what did you put on your list?" she was asked.

"I never did get round to listing them," she replied, "but each time he did something that made me mad, I'd simply say to myself — lucky for him it's one of the ten!"

TUESDAY — AUGUST 24.

GRANDPARENTS are wonderful, aren't they? I thought of them when I read these words by the writer Rachel Carson:

"If a child is to keep alive his inborn sense of wonder . . . he needs the companionship of an adult who can share it, rediscovering the joy, excitement and mystery of the world we live in."

Now, isn't that where grandmothers and grandfathers come in?

WEDNESDAY — AUGUST 25.

LOUISA M. ALCOTT was determined to become an author. Even though an editor had told her father that she would never be successful, she resolved to prove him wrong.

She worked hard but at first failed to gain the hoped-for success. Only after a long time had elapsed did she discover her real talent. It was her mother who advised her to write about family life — her three sisters and their ups-and-downs. The result was "Little Women".

Even then the publisher was doubtful if the book would interest girls, but his niece proved him wrong for she was soon enthralled by the adventures of the March family.

The novel became world famous and it is still popular today. It was persistence that made Louisa carry out her mother's suggestion and probably, like many mothers, Mrs Alcott believed there isn't such a word as "can't!"

THURSDAY — AUGUST 26.

I CAME on these words, sung and spoken by Violeta Parra, the much-loved folksinger from Chile, who died in 1967:

Please do not cry when the sun is gone because, if you do, the tears won't let you see the stars.

There is, don't you think, something quite beautiful as well as inspiring in that thought?

FRIDAY — AUGUST 27.

THE Lady of the House had been to the local flower show, and arrived home in a thoughtful mood.

"Sometimes I wonder if we search too hard for perfection," she mused. "All the blooms were beautiful, and it seemed such a shame that so many failed to win prizes simply because of minor blemishes and faults."

I understood exactly what she meant. Laudable though it is to search for perfection, we should never allow that quest to blind us to the everyday beauty all around us, even if it does have minor flaws — and I'm not just talking about flowers!

SATURDAY — AUGUST 28.

"ABOUT the best way to grow old is not to be in so much of a hurry about it!"

We don't know who wrote those words, attributed to the often very wise Anon. But don't they make a grand thought for today? Somehow I can imagine Anon. writing the words with a twinkle in his or her eye!

RED HEADS

SUNDAY — AUGUST 29.

GRACE to you, and peace, from God our Father and the Lord Jesus Christ.

Philemon 1:3

MONDAY — AUGUST 30.

THAT wise philosopher Lao-zi, who lived in China in the 6th century BC, wrote a book of 5250 words after riding on an ox-drawn chariot to his retirement retreat in the mountains. He had been Keeper Of The Archives in the imperial capital of Loyang. Here are a few of his wise words:

Kindness in words creates confidence.
Kindness in thinking creates profoundness.
Kindness in giving creates love.

TUESDAY — AUGUST 31.

I CAME upon this little verse and found it most appealing. It reminds me of the Sunday school hymn we used to sing, about being "like a little candle burning in the night". Today it seems even more important to spread a little brightness in the world:

Shine like a candle, shine like a star,
Shine at the place, in the space where you are.
Show to the world a face that is bright,
Where there is darkness, let there be light.

May you always find a little brightness and cheerfulness within you and share it with those around you!

September

WEDNESDAY — SEPTEMBER 1.

WHAT is the noblest sight you can think of? A great mountain? A mighty waterfall? A spectacular sunset?

The poet Robert Burns had no doubts on the matter. He gave his opinion in one immortal line: "An honest man's the noblest work of God."

I am sure that today he would have somehow added the words "or woman"!

THURSDAY — SEPTEMBER 2.

I WAS sitting in the garden one evening in late Summer enjoying the last rays of sunshine, when my attention was caught by a bee collecting nectar from a nearby plant.

I was surprised to see it so busy, and all on its own, for it was late in the day and I had already decided that the veronica flowers were over and should be cut back without delay. But the bee knew better and it went systematically from spike to spike until the last drop of nectar had been collected, before flying back to the hive.

Now, if ever I am tempted to give up something that has become difficult or tedious, I think about the bee and the way it persevered in its work — and I determine to keep going as well.

PONY TALE

FRIDAY — SEPTEMBER 3.

THE Welsh Guards were the first troops to enter and liberate the city of Brussels during the Second World War. When the war ended the Guards were invited to return and they were presented with a Gideon (a standard) by the Belgian government, a token of their gratitude for the part played in liberating their capital.

On a cold, sunny day, matched by the warmth of the people crowding all around, a grand ceremony took place. The Mayor of Brussels presented the Standard to the Commanding Officer in the presence of the Belgian King, Queen and family.

The spirits and morale of the soldiers were very high indeed, to the point that they "dressed" the national monument of Brussels in the Welsh Guards' uniform, much to the delight of the locals!

And every year, as a tribute, on 3rd September the little Manneken Pis statue is dressed in the Welsh Guards' uniform of a Sergeant Major, in recognition of the liberation of Brussels by this regiment in 1944.

SATURDAY — SEPTEMBER 4.

HERE are some wise and comforting words to remember, when your personal sky is overcast and grey. They were written by the Victorian poet Robert Browning:

Lo, life again knocked laughing at the door.
The world goes on, goes ever, in and through,
And out again o' the cloud.

SUNDAY — SEPTEMBER 5.

AND he that sat upon the throne said, Behold, I make all things new. And he said unto me, Write: for these words are true and faithful.

Revelation 21:5

MONDAY — SEPTEMBER 6.

WHEN you feel that your life's in confusion,
When your steps seem to slither and slide,
When each road seems to lead to disaster,
Remember — you do have a Guide.

When you feel very small and forsaken,
When you're fearful of terrors unknown,
When you're lost in a land full of strangers,
Remember — you're never alone.

When your world seems o'ershadowed by sorrow,
When you're hurt, or cast down by despair,
Remember — there's Someone who loves you,
Who will keep you throughout in His care.

Margaret Ingall.

TUESDAY — SEPTEMBER 7.

"COME and look — I've a surprise for you," Johnny greeted me. I followed him down an old country track bordering a field ablaze with red poppies to the ruins of an old farm cottage.

In front of us lay a wall of roses, waxy white, yellow and deep red, climbing over the gable end of the ruins. The families who lived there and had planted those flowers were long since gone, but they'd left a lasting legacy.

WEDNESDAY — SEPTEMBER 8.

WHEN The Lady of the House and I called in to visit Carol, we found her at home with her feet up.

"I had such a busy day yesterday," she told me. "My granddaughter's class visited a nature reserve, and I went along as a helper. The children learned a lot from the guide, but I think I learned even more from the children.

"You see," she explained, "I'd stopped noticing just how beautiful a shiny new conker can be, just how wonderful is the smell of damp woodland, and just what fun it is to hear the wind whistling through the trees overhead, and watch the leaves whirling down all around you. It was a real joy to be reminded of such simple delights."

Isn't it lucky that a childlike wonder is so infectious — I'm sure it does us all good to catch a dose of it sometimes!

THURSDAY — SEPTEMBER 9.

I SELDOM like to rush into what people call "spur-of-the-moment" decisions or actions. It is wise to be well briefed on the things you plan to do, and that's why these words appealed when a friend quoted them to me:

"Sometimes the most important thing in a whole day is the rest we take between two deep breaths."

In other words, take time, no matter how briefly, to consider what you are about to do. And, yes, do think before you speak.

YOUNG
EXPLORER

FRIDAY — SEPTEMBER 10.

I WAS delighted one Sunday to hear a preacher, talking on the subject of perfection, admit that he himself had failed at times to follow a tradition that made it imperative for him to search for perfection in all things. The great lesson of his sermon was that, in fact, God places no such impossible burdens on us.

He asks us only to be ourselves, with all our strengths and weaknesses and, of course, to accept them in others. When things don't go so well for us, we are encouraged to help each other and learn through our mistakes.

Thank goodness He is always there to help us.

SATURDAY — SEPTEMBER 11.

TAKE a moment today to tell someone you know how much you appreciate them but have somehow forgotten to tell them. Say thank you now for that recent good deed, that kindly thought by friend or stranger.

Tragedies strike both at personal and international level and at such times we realise how seldom we tell our loved ones just how much they mean to us.

A "hug" can say a thousand words.

SUNDAY — SEPTEMBER 12.

I CRIED unto God with my voice, even unto God with my voice; and he gave ear unto me.

Psalms 77:1

MONDAY — SEPTEMBER 13.

YOUNG Gemma looked innocent enough when she asked me if I knew which was the longest word in the dictionary. But when I confessed I didn't she broke into a grin.

"It's 'smiles'," she told me triumphantly, "because there's a mile between the first and last letters!"

I had to laugh with her, but it did occur to me that there was perhaps more than a grain of sense in her answer. A smile may not last a literal mile, but it can certainly go a long way towards making the world a pleasanter place!

TUESDAY — SEPTEMBER 14.

THE weather was really wild that morning but Nell decided to go for a walk, anyway. The sound of the crash of the waves on the shore and the feel of the wind in her face added excitement to her routine constitutional, and she thoroughly enjoyed braving the elements knowing that a hot bath and comfortable sofa were only minutes away.

As she walked she began to think about those who battle storms in their lives every day. When such storms take the form of illness or bereavement, thoughts of a cosy fireside aren't enough — that's when the warmth of friendship can provide some shelter from the worst of the weather.

Your helping hand can be an umbrella to break the force of the storm.

WEDNESDAY — SEPTEMBER 15.

IN the north of Scotland water lilies grow on many lochs. They stand in such stark contrast to the tremendous power of the dark hills and woods above them. Their white hearts open to the sunlight in exquisite expressions of Summer beauty.

Yet you will never be able to reach out from the loch edge to pick one. That can be guaranteed. Water lilies are always tantalisingly just out of reach, a fraction beyond our fingers.

These beautiful floating blooms are a perfect reminder that much of what is best in life is there for us all to share and enjoy — not for one individual to snatch and monopolise.

THURSDAY — SEPTEMBER 16.

A BRIGHT and blessed thing to see,
The lovely laden apple tree.
From the lowest branches I take
Four apples for my childhood's sake:
One that I may remember still
The Spring's first yellow daffodil;
One for high Summer; bathed in light
The great elms quiver in my sight;
One for the harvest, Autumn's crown,
When rough hands lay the sickles down;
And one for when the Winter rain
Will sweep the upland and the plain.
My lovely fruitful apple tree
Spells out the seasons — just for me.

Glynfab John.

FRIDAY — SEPTEMBER 17.

TIME FLIES

WHATEVER happened to Monday?
It simply melted away,
And every week seems to vanish —
It's due to age, they say!
I remember places I have been
And faces I used to know,
But Tuesday, Wednesday and Thursday,
Gone like the melted snow.

So then it's Friday once again,
With the weekend drawing near,
And Sunday can be wonderful,
Or boring, dull and drear.
And so the months keep slipping by
And the years will not relent,
Whatever happened to Monday?
It simply came and went!

Iris Hesselden.

SATURDAY — SEPTEMBER 18.

I THOROUGHLY enjoyed reading an article by a lady ninety years young about her adventures. These included Christmas dinner in the most unlikely places and a very bumpy flight over the infamous Bermuda Triangle.

She came to live in our country from abroad about five years ago and has since made a whole new life for herself. As the saying goes, "It's not how old you are, but how you are old!"

MOTHER EARTH

SUNDAY — SEPTEMBER 19.

TO him be glory and dominion for ever and ever. Amen.

Peter I 5:11

MONDAY — SEPTEMBER 20.

THE Rev Brian Brown was one of many missionaries trying to give practical help to refugees and victims of war in many different parts of Africa. Sometimes it seemed very hard work, but at other times something was said or done which made it all worthwhile. One of the leaders in Sierra Leone once said:

"Reverend, I am an old man and I am a Muslim. I will die as a Muslim. But there are many young people in this refugee camp. They see how Chrisitians have brought rice and oil. They see how you have helped us to build our homes. They will decide what religion to follow. But this we all know — you have a great and a good God."

Rev Brown reflected that in the early days of the Christian church it had been said: "See how these Christians love one another." That elderly man had said something even more wonderful: 'See how these Christians love those who are not Christians'."

TUESDAY — SEPTEMBER 21.

HERE'S something to think about today, the words of a centuries-old Japanese proverb:

Vision without action is a daydream,
Action without vision is a nightmare.

WEDNESDAY — SEPTEMBER 22.

I LIKE the story of the mother long ago whose little girl was afraid to go to sleep in the dark. Then one night her mother suddenly had an idea.

She placed a candle by her child's bed and told her, "All the darkness in the world cannot put out that candle. It will protect you all night long."

From then on the child slept peacefully and without fear.

THURSDAY — SEPTEMBER 23.

RECIPE FOR FRIENDSHIP

TAKE a large supply of tolerance
and sprinkle it with care,
Stir in dependability
with willingness to share,

Make a roux of staunchness
and marinate for years,
Then add reliability
(discarding any tears).

Fold in a heap of readiness
to lend a helping hand,
Blend it all together
and forever let it stand,

Bake in the Summer sunshine,
preserve in Winter snow,
A recipe for friendship
to make your spirit glow.

Brian Hope Gent.

FRIDAY — SEPTEMBER 24.

ARE you the kind of person who tackles too much, sometimes beyond your capabilities? A desire to reach for the stars, to attempt something difficult and remote, is all very well, but often hard to achieve. Here are two pieces of advice tailor-made for you:

"Work within your abilities. Do not let what you cannot do interfere with what you can do."
John Wooden.

"I have learnt that I am me, that I can do the things that, as one might put it, me can do, but I cannot do the things that me would like to do."
Agatha Christie.

SATURDAY — SEPTEMBER 25.

VISITORS to the Cartmel area of Grange-over-Sands often climb up to a square building with a railed roof. From this edifice, Hampsfell Hospice, they obtain magnificent views of some Lakeland mountains, including Coniston Old Man and Helvellyn. There are views of the Morecambe and Heysham areas to the south.

This viewpoint was a favourite of the Rev. Thomas Rimmington, a local clergyman. So deeply did he love it that he had the building erected so that other people could enjoy the pleasure of the scenery, long after his death. On the walls of the building visitors can enjoy some of his poetry. One quotation reads:

This Hospice has an open door
Alike it welcomes rich and poor.

SUNDAY — SEPTEMBER 26.

HE that loveth his brother abideth in the light, and there is none occasion of stumbling in him.

John I 2:10

MONDAY — SEPTEMBER 27.

THE more that we are friendly,
the less will be our care,
The less we grouse and grumble,
the more content we'll share.
The less we fret and worry,
the more we'll come to find
That happiness is more or less
for everyone designed.

Thomas Hood.

TUESDAY — SEPTEMBER 28.

WHEN Maggie's neighbour caught flu, it was only reluctantly that she volunteered to take over the job of walking his dog. At the time it seemed just another chore to be added to an already busy schedule but, to her surprise, she soon found herself seeing it in quite another light.

"That interlude of fresh air and exercise became a real pleasure," she said. "I revisited almost forgotten parts of my neighbourhood, and talked to folk I never usually see. Now, whether or not the dog comes with me, I still try to fit that half-hour walk into my day."

All of us need time to ourselves; what better way to spend it than enjoying the world around us?

WEDNESDAY — SEPTEMBER 29.

WHEN Abraham Lincoln was a young man, it was said of him: "Lincoln has nothing, only plenty of friends."

Perhaps it is worth remembering that to have lots of friends is to be very rich indeed. We can all be wealthy in this sense if we value and nurture our friendships . . . not forgetting the best Friend of all!

THURSDAY — SEPTEMBER 30.

PETER'S grandfather had almost forgotten just how dirty the old steam engines were. Waiting on the platform in the wind and the rain, he remembered his boyhood holidays and said a silent thank you for diesel trains and motor cars.

However, this outing wasn't for his benefit, but for young Peter. The tiny station was crowded with train enthusiasts and volunteer staff, and a great sense of enjoyment could be felt. Eventually, the train arrived and a huge cloud of steam and smoke enveloped the passengers as they rushed towards the carriages. At the other end, there were more enthusiasts, more cameras and more noise.

Some two hours later, after tea and orange squash, Grandfather at last made his escape. There had been little opportunity to talk, but he only had to look at Peter's face to see that the afternoon had been a great success. The little boy had a dirty face, grubby hands and a beaming smile.

Nothing can ever replace the magic of steam!

October

FRIDAY — OCTOBER 1.

WELCOME TO AUTUMN

THE Summer may be over
And Winter drawing near,
But now it's time for meetings,
For friendship, warmth and cheer.
There's purple on the mountains
And beauty all around,
With here and there a Summer rose
Still waiting to be found.

It's time for reminiscing,
Recalling Summer days,
For sharing hope and happy thoughts
In many quiet ways.
A time of relaxation
Of fellowship and joy,
Creating Autumn memories
That Winter can't destroy.

Iris Hesselden.

SATURDAY — OCTOBER 2.

"SOME of your griefs you have cured, and the sharpest you have survived; but what torments of pain you endured, from evils that never arrived."

Ralph Waldo Trine.

SUNDAY — OCTOBER 3.

WHO is this King of glory? The Lord of hosts, he is the King of glory.
Psalms 24:10

MONDAY — OCTOBER 4.

TALKING POINT

IF birds and bees,
And rocks and trees,
And listening walls could speak;
Then history would likely be
Re-written in a week.

TUESDAY— OCTOBER 5.

MUCH as our friend Robert enjoys his garden, he admits that he always finds the annual Autumn tidy-up to be a slightly melancholy affair.

It may be satisfying to see the vegetable plot and flower-beds restored to order, but it is certainly rather sad to look at the empty spaces where once the earth was flourishing with Summer blooms and produce.

The Lady of the House commented, "Remember that by getting rid of this year's old stock, Robert's giving next year's plants a chance to grow."

Her wise words reminds us just how often we discover that it's only by clearing out the weeds and dead wood from our hearts and minds that we can find the room for our own new spiritual growth.

WEDNESDAY — OCTOBER 6.

HARRY had been invited to a wedding and, when I called by, he was busy poring over a list of suggested presents for the engaged couple.

"I don't know," he said, scratching his head. "It's at times like this that I really take my hat off to God. We never have to bother about choosing what sort of gifts we are born with, yet somehow we seem to enter the world with the things that we need to enrich our lives.

"Now, if only I could give Simon and Emily the gift of tolerance, the gift of seeing the funny side of life and the gift of being able to enjoy every day as it comes — why then, they really would be presents worth having."

I had to agree; what a shame that they aren't to be found in the shops!

THURSDAY — OCTOBER 7.

IN the Jewish faith they celebrate the New Year in the Autumn, which may seem strange. At this feast of Rosh Hashanah they believe that God opens a book in which He writes everyone's destiny for the coming year.

For the following ten days, Jews reflect on their lives and their commitment to the Lord and to their neighbours, then the book is closed. It reminds me of the season of Lent which gives Christians a time to meditate on our faith.

Two different religions, both united by devoting a special time to think about the nature of God and His love.

FRIDAY — OCTOBER 8.

SAM was busy in his greenhouse one day. "Don't sneeze!" he warned me, only half-jokingly. "I've just opened a packet of Icelandic poppy seeds, and they're so tiny that even the slightest movement of the air could scatter them."

I peered over his shoulder, awed that such minuscule specks as seeds can hold within them all the things necessary to grow into plants. And once again I was reminded that even though we can often seem tiny and insignificant, we, too, are filled with the potential for greatness.

It's a thought worth hanging on to when we seem too small to ever make our mark.

SATURDAY — OCTOBER 9.

I CAME across these lines, author unknown, and I'd like to pass them on to you today:

I wish I were big enough honestly to admit all
my shortcomings;
Brilliant enough to accept praise without it
making me arrogant;
Tall enough to tower above deceit;
Strong enough to welcome criticism;
Compassionate enough to understand
human frailties;
Wise enough to recognise my mistakes;
Humble enough to appreciate greatness;
Staunch enough to stand by my friends;
Human enough to be thoughtful of my neighbours,
And righteous enough to be devoted to the
love of God.

SUNDAY — OCTOBER 10.

HUMBLE yourselves in the sight of the Lord, and he shall lift you up.

James 4:10

MONDAY — OCTOBER 11.

IN a way, life can be said to be like a football match . . .

Any attack by pessimism should be tackled vigorously, and never be allowed to play a major role.

Optimism and fortitude can provide a strong defence, whenever adversity tries to dribble its way through.

Intolerant tactics must be regarded as foul play, and there will be a penalty to pay if lethargy makes its presence felt.

Ungentlemanly conduct quite rightly deserves a red card.

Points can be won by honest endeavour, and the best results can be achieved simply by keeping an eye on the ball until the final whistle blows.

It's a goal worth celebrating!

TUESDAY — OCTOBER 12.

HERE'S a thought for a day in which the going, as they say, may be getting a little troublesome.

The American actor James Dean once told friends: "I can't change the direction of the wind, but I can adjust my sails to always reach my destination."

Now, isn't that something worth pondering on?

GUARDIAN OF
THE LAND

WEDNESDAY — OCTOBER 13.

WE'VE known Ron for many years now, and are always glad to see him whenever he calls by. He's a gregarious chap, and when The Lady of the House once complimented him on his large circle of friends, he grinned a little sheepishly.

"It wasn't always the case," he admitted. "You see, when I was a young man, and bought my first house, it needed quite a lot of attention. I set to work, determined to make my new abode the envy of all the street. I hammered and sawed, painted and papered, refusing all offers of help, because I didn't trust anyone to do the job to my own high standards.

"When, months later, I finally finished, I decided to give a housewarming party — only to realise that I had hardly any friends left to invite!" He laughed ruefully. "It was painful at the time, but it did teach me a valuable lesson. No project is more important than people. Or, as Samuel Johnson put it: 'A man, sir, should keep his friendship in constant repair.'"

Now that's one maintenance task that I'm always happy to carry out!

THURSDAY — OCTOBER 14.

"IN all things do your best. The man who has done his best has done everything. The man who has done less than his best has done nothing."

Charles Schwab.

FRIDAY — OCTOBER 15.

ONE Sunday morning I met Tommy, an elderly neighbour, who was obviously in high spirits. He said he was celebrating not winning a lottery prize. At first I thought I had misheard him, but then he explained that on the night of the draw all the family sat round the television discussing what they would do if they won a large prize.

He wanted to go on a world cruise but his wife Christine, who dislikes water said he could go on his own! His daughter Paula, who is shortly to be married, said he could buy her a new house but his older son John, objected, saying that he had managed to raise his own family without financial support.

So it was quite a relief when Tommy discovered that they had won nothing and the dissent died down. They are a very happy, close-knit family and Tommy believes that is because they have always had to work hard together to get on; he is convinced that sudden wealth might loosen the family links!

SATURDAY — OCTOBER 16.

THE Japanese have a time-honoured proverb which deserves to be quoted: "Fall seven times — stand up eight!"

This is surely another version of the words of that wise philosopher Confucius, who said: "Our greatest glory is not in never falling but in rising every time we fall."

SUNDAY — OCTOBER 17.

JESUS saith unto her, I that speak unto thee am he.

John 4:26

MONDAY — OCTOBER 18.

I USED to know a devout Welshman whose cottage on a remote stretch of the coast commanded a fine view over the sea. Once, he beckoned me across to the window to watch a magnificent flaming sunset.

"Look at that!" he said. "All day, out there, God's sun was warming my body, but now it is warming my soul."

TUESDAY — OCTOBER 19.

LIFE is like a road map.
Of that, there's little doubt,
Revealing some connections
If we care to look about.

Though routes may tend to vary,
What a difference it can make,
By knowing which direction
It's sensible to take.

So let's navigate life's road map
With a willingness to stress
We hope to join the tail-back
On the road to happiness.

John M. Robertson.

WEDNESDAY — OCTOBER 20.

SOMETIMES one person's misfortune can actually bring help to others. There have been many examples when illness in a family has resulted in someone devoting their energy to helping others similarly afflicted, or in fund-raising for a particular organisation.

I am reminded of a young clergyman's wife who was taken ill in a supermarket and was rushed to hospital for an operation. With two small children at home, help was needed urgently. Church friends rallied round and formed a rota to look after the family and take care of cooking, washing and cleaning.

When the young mother recovered, she realised that there must be a lot of others in the same situation. She decided to keep the scheme going, and so "Mothers In Need" was born.

It was advertised in the parish magazine and in the doctor's surgery, giving contact phone numbers. Now it is well established, with a team of volunteers. And what a lifeline it has been!

THURSDAY — OCTOBER 21.

ONE day, the Lady of the House received a beautiful card from a friend in the United States. Since it wasn't her birthday, Christmas or Easter, it was thus doubly welcome. The message it conveyed said it all in a few words:

"Just to say I'm thinking of you."

Perhaps there is someone to whom you could send a similar greeting today?

FRIDAY — OCTOBER 22.

HAVE you come across these definitions of a friend?

A friend is someone who ignores your broken fence and admires the flowers in your garden.

True friends are like good books, you don't see them every day but you know where to find them when you need them.

SATURDAY — OCTOBER 23.

DR William Barclay had a fund of good stories and here is one I particularly like.

A former Duke Of Norfolk happened to be at the railway station when a young Irish girl arrived, carrying a heavy bag. She had come to work as a maid at the castle. He watched her as she tried to persuade a porter to carry her luggage to the castle a mile away, offering him a shilling which was all the money she had. The porter contemptuously refused. The Duke, looking shabby as usual, stepped forward, took the girl's bag and walked beside her along the road, talking as they went.

At the end of the journey they went their separate ways. It wasn't until later when she met her employer that the girl knew the Duke Of Norfolk had helped her out — and she had tipped him a shilling! As Dr Barclay concluded:

"It is never safe to judge a person by externals. A great person is always a thoughtful person. The truly great man does not think of his place or his prestige."

SUNDAY — OCTOBER 24.

AS ye have therefore received Christ Jesus the Lord, so walk ye in him. Colossians 2:6

MONDAY — OCTOBER 25.

WE all make mistakes, of course we do. The great thing is to remember not to give any encores.

TUESDAY — OCTOBER 26.

YEARS ago I attempted to paint in oils. I enjoyed it very much, but real talent seemed to be missing. However, the experience taught me a great deal about colour and since then I've learned to look at the world differently.

Long after I'd put away my paints and brushes, I would notice shades and shadows which I wouldn't have seen previously.

Colour is all around us, even when skies are not bright. City pavements in the rain can be steel grey, the road, a ribbon of silver blue. The pools of water have their own rainbows where oil and petrol have dripped. In the countryside, the bracken and trees are still beautiful, with touches of green and russet, black and brown.

When someone says to you: "What miserable weather we're having", don't you believe it. Think of the colours in a paintbox, look around and you will find them.

Nature never puts away her palette or her brushes.

WEDNESDAY — OCTOBER 27.

OUR young friend, Chris, has a word for her 11-year-old son Ben — "invincible". Well, at least he used to think that he was! — vice-captain of the cricket team, a member of the rugby and football teams and nominated several times as "pupil of the week". There seemed to be no stopping him.

However, at the start of the school holidays, whilst playing football, Ben broke his thumb. Six weeks without sport. Those had to be the worst school holidays ever!

Ben has now settled into a new school and is back to his beloved games, but things are not the same, of course. There's a lot of homework for one thing and he doesn't feel quite so important any more.

Aren't we grown-ups very much like that? We stride along with head in the air, ready to take on the world. Yet now and then, the world fights back and cuts us down to size. Occasionally we need to be reminded that, like Ben, we can't always be "invincible".

THURSDAY — OCTOBER 28.

BE still and let your thoughts just drift
But keep your aims in sight
And know always, with God's great help,
Dark worries will take flight.

Jenny Chaplin.

FRIDAY — OCTOBER 29.

GREG GUIRARD, who lives in Louisiana, has acquired an international reputation for his writing and photography, and I think he is also to be admired greatly for another project.

In the 19th century, loggers cut down cypress trees in the forest, and in the early 20th century, when his grandfather had a sawmill, he, too, went on felling without a thought of replanting.

On his grandfather's death, Greg inherited 100 acres, growing sugar cane and corn. In recent years he has been turning these acres back to forest, planting 30,000 trees of 15 varieties.

"One day, it will be a haven for wildlife and a place where people can seek out peace and tranquillity," he says.

What a wonderful dedication to conservation! Perhaps, in our own small corner, we could also become guardians of our own environment.

Mighty oaks from little acorns grow.

SATURDAY — OCTOBER 30.

"GOD gave us two ends. One to sit on and one to think with. Success depends on which one you use; heads you win — tails, you lose."

Now, isn't that an amusing thought to get us motivated?

SUNDAY — OCTOBER 31.

FOR ye know what commandments we gave you by the Lord Jesus. Thessalonians I 4:2

November

MONDAY — NOVEMBER 1.

AS I walked down the street I noticed Angus standing by his front gate surveying the world with satisfaction. "Isn't this just a grand time of year?" he greeted me.

"You like it?" I asked, surprised. "Not many people would pick November as their favourite month."

"Ah, but think of all the good things." He grinned. "The trees alive with colour, buttered toast by the fireside, blackberry jam, and — best of all — no more lawn-mowing until the Spring."

I laughed. Blessings come in many forms, so why not appreciate every one of them!

TUESDAY — NOVEMBER 2.

PHRASE-GAZE

"*MAKING mountains out of mole-hills"*
Is a phrase we often hear
Whenever situations
Involving stress appear.
Yet here's another phrase that may
Assist us all through time,
"Make mole-hills out of mountains" —
They're much easier to climb.

John M. Robertson.

WEDNESDAY — NOVEMBER 3.

SOMEONE once said that what you look for in people is what you find. Look for the bad and it will reveal itself. Look for the good and there it will be.

I don't know if it always works or not, but don't you think it's worth trying? So let's make an effort to look for the best in everyone we meet today!

THURSDAY — NOVEMBER 4.

"NOW, don't overdo it, Dad," said Nicola as her father began to dig the vegetable patch. Such warnings reminded him of his age, yet were kindly meant. "They'll have me permanently stuck in my armchair, carpet slippers on my feet, long before my time," he muttered.

And yet with just a little motivation he could still achieve wonders. It reminded me of the story about the old toad and the young rabbit — the toad was in a deep rut when the rabbit lolloped by.

"What are you doing down there?" asked the rabbit.

"Can't get out," replied the toad.

Later, when the rabbit was returning to his burrow, he met the toad on the side of the road. "I thought you couldn't get out," said the rabbit.

"I couldn't," replied the toad, "but I heard a lorry coming along and I had to!"

It's surprising what we can achieve when we really have to, isn't it? And a little encouragement makes all the difference.

FRIDAY — NOVEMBER 5.

BONFIRE

I'D like to build a bonfire
And ask the human race
To bring along its clutter
And pile it into place.

We'd heap it with our misdeeds,
Our hatred and our fears,
And all the petty grudges that
We've clung to through the years.

We'd fling on spite and malice,
And ugly gossip, too,
Then watch the flames rise higher
As they burned the rubbish through.

And when at last the ashes
Grew cool and blew away
How shining bright would be the world,
How glorious the day.

Margaret Ingall.

SATURDAY — NOVEMBER 6.

NOWADAYS, I'm glad to say, most husbands help with the washing-up after a meal. In North America they speak about "wiping" the dishes and have a saying, "Wash and wipe together, live in peace together."

It's a belief the Lady of the House thoroughly approves of — and so, I hasten to add, do I!

TURNING
POINT

SUNDAY — NOVEMBER 7.

MY love be with you all in Christ Jesus. Amen.

Corinthians I 16:24

MONDAY — NOVEMBER 8.

IN November, a month of ever-shortening days, we can see the first real frosts of Winter, even snow on the high hills.

But around mid-month there can also be calm, mellow days of pleasant, warm sunshine, and soft blue skies. Days when being outdoors raises the spirits. Days which have long been called St Martin's Summer, and which echo October's St Luke's Little Summer.

Remember, too, that November is the month of saints. The month begins with All Saints' Day on the 1st, when there is a general celebration of saints, and ends on the 30th with the celebration of St Andrew's Day commemorating the patron saint of Scotland.

St Martin, a 4th-century bishop of Tours celebrates his day on November 11th. St Martin gave his name to St Martin's Summer, days which are jewels in the crown of the mature year.

TUESDAY — NOVEMBER 9.

I HAVE a notebook filled with happy thoughts and quotes about the essence of friendship. Here is one I spotted recently on a board at the entrance to a village church:

"Friends are God's way of taking care of us."

I don't think anybody could put it better.

WEDNESDAY — NOVEMBER 10.

WE thank You, Lord for many things,
The blessings of each day,
For home and food and family
And guidance on life's way.
We thank You for the earth and sky,
The beauty all around,
And things we take for granted, Lord,
The gifts of sight and sound.

We pray for those less fortunate
And those who lost their way,
For those in trouble and despair,
Lord, care for them this day.
We thank You for Your wonders, Lord,
Below us and above,
But most of all for hope and faith,
And Your undying love.

Iris Hesselden.

THURSDAY — NOVEMBER 11.

IN this day and age it would sometimes be easy to believe that being successful is all that matters. However, that great genius, Albert Einstein, knew better. He once gave this advice:

"Don't try to become a man of success, but rather try to become a man of value."

That is so much more important.

FRIDAY — NOVEMBER 12.

OUR friend Janice's church is raising money to repair some of the very old stained-glass windows and to install guards to protect them from future damage. The funny thing about church windows is that from the outside they can look rather drab, almost colourless, with nothing about them to attract attention. It is not until we see them from inside with the light shining through them that their full beauty and colour is revealed.

It's rather like folk, I suspect. Perhaps the new arrival in our neighbourhood who doesn't seem inclined to be friendly may be shy, busy or feeling unsettled. We can't always go by appearances. Thankfully, first impressions are not always lasting impressions — just like the stained-glass windows.

SATURDAY — NOVEMBER 13.

DURING the Second World War Vera Lynn's singing of "There'll Be Bluebirds Over The White Cliffs Of Dover" won the people's hearts. Here are the lines which I love the best:

And Jimmy will go to sleep
In his own little bed again.

They remind me of all the little Jimmys — and Jennys — who were sent away as evacuees to live with strangers far from their own homes. And the children who spent night after night in deep, dark air-raid shelters.

Poignant memories indeed for so many.

SUNDAY — NOVEMBER 14.

SET your affection on things above, not on things on the earth. Colossians 3:2

MONDAY — NOVEMBER 15.

TONY is a keen amateur yachtsman, so when I called in to see him it seemed appropriate that the coffee mug he handed me bore the legend, "A smooth sea never made a skilful sailor".

"A friend of mine bought that for me," he explained. "I like it because the words are so true — not just about sailing, of course, but about the whole of life."

I'm sure he is right. We should always remember that although rough seas may not be much fun to navigate, the experience gained is often invaluable — and what's more, always enhances the pleasure of reaching calmer, safer waters!

TUESDAY — NOVEMBER 16.

DAVID Campbell is a storyteller. He delights his audiences with many tales from history and folklore, and so helps to preserve them.

He has said, "The sound of a word lasts only as long as the breath it makes, but the picture it creates in a listener's mind can be remembered for years."

We, too, can leave pictures in the minds of others. Let's be sure they are lovely to look at.

WEDNESDAY — NOVEMBER 17.

SUNDAY by Sunday, for many years, the parishioners of Little Ness in Shropshire worshipped in their small village church without realising that the four pictures above the altar were immensely valuable.

A new incumbent with an interest in art called in experts and they were found to be German altar panels dating from 1519 valued at £500,000. The church was given permission to sell the panels at auction.

An allocation was set aside for the maintenance of the fabric of the three churches in the united benefice, a further amount was given to the Shropshire Historic Churches Fund, and the biggest share was to go towards a scheme for low-cost housing for villagers.

As Rev. Robin Bradbury said at the time, "We wanted to sell to make sure the pictures were cared for responsibly and we saw the possibility that something good and creative could come out of the sale. This way we shall be investing in people's lives and communities."

THURSDAY — NOVEMBER 18.

HERE are a few words for us to think about as we go about our daily life:

"Don't wish it was easier; wish you were better. Don't wish for fewer problems; wish for more skills. Don't wish for fewer challenges; wish for more wisdom."

These words were written by Jim Rohn.

FRIDAY — NOVEMBER 19.

AT the beginning of the 18th century anyone passing Elgin Cathedral might have noticed a rather eccentric-looking man busily clearing away rubbish. He was, in fact, a local shoemaker who had often been frowned on by the local authorities.

One influential man, in 1824, had the bright idea of appointing John Shanks as Keeper Of The Cathedral. So well was this belief justified that John went on to serve the cathedral for 25 years.

In that time it was reported that he cleared away 3000 barrowloads of rubbish. No forklift or modern equipment for him, but sheer hard physical toil. Not only did he work diligently but, by example, inspired others to help restore the historic building and its surroundings.

This demonstrates what can be achieved by someone who at first seems an unlikely candidate, but goes on to prove that another's faith in him or her has not been misplaced.

SATURDAY — NOVEMBER 20.

THERE is a lovely Indian belief that everyone is a house with four rooms. One is physical, one mental, one emotional and one — perhaps most important of all — spiritual.

To live a complete life, the belief goes on, we should visit each room every day and open the window to keep it aired and fresh.

The Photographers

Marcello Aita;
The Door Is Always Open.

David Bigwood;
Children's Hour.

Jacqui Cordingley;
A Guiding Hand, Quiet Reflection.

Paul Felix;
Turning Point.

V.K. Guy;
Nature's Power, Branching Out, Deep And Crisp And Even, Island Of Dreams.

C.R. Kilvington;
Mother Earth.

Douglas Laidlaw;
Pony Tale, Young Explorer.

Malcolm Nash;
Steadfast.

Oakleaf;
Scene At The Shore, Where The Heart Is.

Polly Pullar;
Cosy Corner.

Clifford Robinson;
Ideal Home.

Willie Shand;
Shadow Of The Cross, The Green Grass Of Home, Floral Tribute, Red Heads.

S. W. Images;
Good Companions, Earth's Treasure, Guardian Of The Land.

Sheila Taylor;
House And Garden, Bonnie Banks, Resting Place.

Richard Watson;
Winter Blanket, Full Steam Ahead.

Printed and Published by D. C. Thomson & Co., Ltd.,
185 Fleet Street, London EC4A 2HS.

ISBN 0-85116-834-5

WEDNESDAY — DECEMBER 29.

WHAT a difference a smile makes! These lines surely say it all:

A cheery smile each joy will double,
And cut in half your every trouble.

THURSDAY — DECEMBER 30.

I SELDOM end a year without thinking that life is an intertwining of joy and sorrow, each setting off the other to make, on the whole, a rather lovely and memorable tapestry. This thought was shared, I think, by the 18th-century poet Alexander Pope, who wrote:

Love, hope, and joy, fair pleasure's smiling train,
Hate, fear, and grief, the family of pain,
These mix'd with art, and to due bounds confin'd,
Make and maintain the balance of the mind;
The lights and shades, whose well accorded strife
Gives all the strength and colour to our life.

FRIDAY — DECEMBER 31.

ON New Year's Eve we like to leave
Another year behind,
And gaze into the future,
Little knowing what we'll find;
But let us hope that proper scope
Is organised to rear
Optimistic options
In the coming year.

J. M. Robertson.

SUNDAY — DECEMBER 26.

NOW when Jesus was born in Bethlehem of Judæa in the days of Herod the king, behold, there came wise men from the east to Jerusalem. Matthew 2:1

MONDAY — DECEMBER 27.

OUR friend Elizabeth loves rambling, and often makes up rhymes as she walks. This one, she told us, was composed to encourage herself up one particularly steep hillside:

Everyone has to start somewhere,
No matter how daunting the slope
Though your spirits may sink to your bootstraps
And you may feel you simply won't cope —
But take just one step, then another,
Just a pace at a time, taking care,
And then, when you look for the summit
You'll suddenly find that you're there!

Words to remember when facing a challenge!

TUESDAY — DECEMBER 28.

AS the year draws to a close, here is a thought for today — and all the days to come.

"Don't be too busy, too serious, too sensible — at least, not all the time! Remember to have a little fun, enjoy a little nonsense, a sprinkling of dreams, even a few daydreams, to balance life's doing. Make the most, too, of life's small joys and pleasures as well as its great happinesses. It will help you to cope all the better with the ups and downs of life!"

ISLAND OF
DREAMS

FRIDAY — DECEMBER 24.

I KNOW it isn't easy, but Cardinal Newman once said that we should treat an enemy as if he would one day be our friend.

As I say, it isn't easy, but who wants to keep an enemy? Even one is one too many. But we can never have too many friends.

SATURDAY — DECEMBER 25.

CHRISTMAS is for children —
See their faces glow.
See their bright eyes sparkle
At the hint of snow!

Hear them singing carols
Round a Christmas tree.
Watch them open presents,
Wrapped in mystery.

Listen to their laughter,
Share their joy and mirth.
With the hearts of children
Celebrate Christ's birth.

Share their festive pleasures,
Join their cheerful song.
Shower them with good things —
Childhood's not for long.

Children of all ages
Christmas greet with glee,
And though Time brings changes
May it always be.

Glynfab John.

WEDNESDAY — DECEMBER 22.

HOW much, I sometimes wonder, will we remember of today when the sun has gone down and these twenty-four hours have been consigned to the part of the week we know as yesterday?

The Italian writer Cesare Pavese surely caught time in perspective when he said: "We never remember the days, but we always remember the moments."

How right he was! It is always those all too short hours, minutes, even a few seconds of happiness, which stay in our minds long after each day has gone.

THURSDAY — DECEMBER 23.

I LIKE the unusual variation on this theme which I came across in an old book. Someone was talking about the Christmas song, "I saw three ships . . ."

What are those three ships? Well, the first is worship — remember that the Wise Men fell down and worshipped;

The second is friendship — remember that Christmas should be a time for making new friendships and strengthening old ones;

The third is stewardship — remember that a steward is one who serves and helps his fellow man.

My informant concluded, "May these three ships sail into our hearts and homes this Christmas."

SUNDAY — DECEMBER 19.

AND this shall be a sign unto you; Ye shall find the babe wrapped in swaddling clothes, lying in a manger.

Luke 2:12

MONDAY — DECEMBER 20.

MARTHA is a would-be writer, and frequently enters short story and poetry competitions, although not always successfully. I once asked her if she ever became disheartened.

"Occasionally," she admitted, "but never for long. When I was small, my mother taught me this rhyme, and I've always found it inspiring:

It's hard to meet with failure as if we do not mind,
For failure wears a gloomy face: his aspect is unkind.
But yet if we're courageous, and greet him with a will
We'll find he is a teacher of unexpected skill.
And when at last, as time goes by, and failure goes away,
We often find we're stronger than before he came to stay.

TUESDAY — DECEMBER 21.

IT'S that memory-filled time of the year when we go in search of a beautiful thought for the season. Here's one of my favourites:

"If Christmas isn't found in your heart, you won't find it under the tree!"

DEEP AND CRISP
AND EVEN

FRIDAY — DECEMBER 17.

A FRIEND was on holiday in California and, while walking through the little town called Eureka, she copied this poem which was written on an art shop's window pane:

May you always have the art to charm your days,
A sensible hearth and friends as dependable as gravity.
May the wind and creatures be as music to your evenings,
And may your dreams leave you renewed, make you wake to sunlight.
And may your garden fill you with scents and colours,
And may your fence be low enough that you can see your neighbour's smile.

James Bertolino.

Isn't that a touching poem filled with so many things to think about?

SATURDAY — DECEMBER 18.

DO you know why rosemary with its silvery green leaves has flowers of a clear blue?

A great deal of story and legend is often attached to plants, and it is said that, when Mary and Joseph with the baby Jesus were fleeing into Egypt to escape the wrath of King Herod, Mary hung the Christ Child's linen to dry on a sweet-smelling rosemary bush, and from then on the rosemary's white flowers turned to the delicate blue we know today.

WEDNESDAY — DECEMBER 15.

JOHN WATSON was a Presbyterian minister in Liverpool for about fifteen years and under the pen-name Ian Maclaren he wrote his outstandingly-successful books such as "Beside The Bonnie Briar Bush" (1894) and "Days Of Auld Lang Syne" (1895).

He was often accused of being too sentimental by his critics. However, whether living his life as John Watson, church divine, or as Ian Maclaren, the writer, this courageous man kept to his own often-declared principle: "Be kind . . . everybody's fighting a hard battle."

It says it all in a few well-chosen words, doesn't it? Good common sense and compassion for others, with which to keep alive our many friendships on life's journey.

THURSDAY — DECEMBER 16.

MILLIONS of greetings and good wishes flood homes worldwide each December. They come in all shapes and varieties, from the traditional to ultra-modern and are hugely appreciated by the recipients.

Sometimes a simple greeting makes a bigger impression than the wordy and sentimental. I came on these words in a Christmas card which also carried traditional New Year greetings:

We wish you the least of the very worst, and the most of the very best.

The simplest words are often the best.

SUNDAY — DECEMBER 12.

REJOICE in the Lord alway: and again I say, Rejoice.
Philippians 4:4

MONDAY — DECEMBER 13.

SOMETHING happened one day which annoyed our friend Mark a great deal. His wife Patricia told him to calm down and she began to recite:

"Don't make tragedies of trifles,
Don't shoot butterflies with rifles —
Laugh it off!"

An unknown hand wrote this humorous little verse to remind us not to fret or fume over the minor irritations and troubles of life. Those small annoying things pass, and will be forgotten sooner than we think.

Mark later admitted after he had calmed down a bit that he did realise the cause of his irritation was in fact almost comical. He soon began to feel just a little foolish for having made a mountain out of a molehill!

TUESDAY — DECEMBER 14.

WHEN Santa Claus talks to children he always has to be ready for anything. In one store he asked a little boy, "Well, and have you written me a letter to tell me what you would like for Christmas?"

"Didn't you get my e-mail?" came the reply.

FRIDAY — DECEMBER 10.

MICHAEL was only a little boy playing in the streets of Florence, but he was making some beautiful models out of mud and was noticed by Ghirlandajo, one of the city's great artists who was responsible for several frescoes in Florence's churches and farther afield. He invited the boy to his studio in order to study art seriously.

It wasn't long before he had learned all that Ghirlandajo was able to teach him, and went on to the studio of Duke Lorenzo the Magnificent. The boy, very nervous in the presence of another master painter, drew the hands of Ghirlandajo — and thus began a further stage in his artistic career. But he never forgot his old master, and much later in life paid him a visit. He left a package for him to open — a beautiful drawing of those two hands which had been instrumental in teaching the delicate art of drawing.

Ghirlandajo might never have been known to us, had it not been for the gratitude of the little boy he picked up out of the gutter — and who we know best as Michelangelo.

SATURDAY — DECEMBER 11.

HERE is a seasonal thought to keep in mind as the festive season approaches:

"What is Christmas? It is tenderness for the past, courage for the present, hope for the future. It is a fervent wish that every cup may overflow with blessings rich and eternal, and that every path may lead to peace." Agnes M. Pharo.

BRANCHING OUT

WEDNESDAY — DECEMBER 8.

WHILE on her travels one of our friends picked up a leaflet entitled "Mind Your Attitude". She was so impressed with it she passed copies on to all her acquaintances. I'd like to share a little of it with you now:

"Today and every day you have a choice regarding the attitude you are going to embrace. Life, as you know, is 10% what happens to you, and 90% how you react to it. So remember that you are in charge of all your attitudes."

THURSDAY — DECEMBER 9.

HAVE you seen brightly-coloured tulips made out of wood for sale in shops? We saw a colourful display of these in a shop window one day. However, thinking the Lady of the House wasn't fond of artificial flowers, I resisted the temptation to buy them.

A few days later, a friend arrived with a small bunch as a gift. The Lady of the House was so obviously delighted, that when Janet left, I couldn't help remarking that surely she usually preferred fresh flowers.

"Yes, I know," she replied, "but these give such a splash of colour on a grey day. Then, taking out a book of quotations, she read me these words: "In the depths of Winter, I finally learned that within me lay an invincible Summer!"

"I may not be as clever as Albert Camus," she said, "but these little tulips will help to brighten the dull days ahead."

SUNDAY — DECEMBER 5.

HE that hath an ear, let him hear what the Spirit saith unto the churches.

Revelation 3:22

MONDAY — DECEMBER 6.

THE famous writer J. M. Barrie not only thrilled the young at heart with his delightful play "Peter Pan", but also wrote charming essays and made entertaining speeches containing little gems of wisdom. Here is one I want to share with you today:

"Those who bring sunshine into the lives of others cannot keep it from themselves. They make me realise that, though I may not be a sun, I at least can be a candle."

TUESDAY — DECEMBER 7.

WE all know the code letters sometimes used to end a letter or card, or seal an envelope, such as R.S.V.P. and S.W.A.L.K., but I wonder if you know this one? R.S.A.C. They were written below the signature on a card sent to a friend in hospital and did they set a welcome challenge as she tried to decipher them!

"It certainly kept my mind off my aches and pains," Irene said.

In fact, the initials mean: "Remember Someone Always Cares".

Perhaps you could use this one yourself next time you write a special letter or card.

FRIDAY — DECEMBER 3.

SOME of our most meaningful thoughts and ideas date back into history, and are the better for having stood the test of time. Here's an example, an old proverb from Denmark, which I found in a book of quotes:

"The road to a friend's house is never long."

A cheering thought, indeed, in any language.

SATURDAY — DECEMBER 4.

FLOWERS have long been associated with expressions of affection towards another person in times of illness or sorrow, or in times of great joy such as weddings. In the language of flowers, many blooms have a special meaning.

In Victorian times, ladies were particularly conscious of this. A circular bridal bouquet of all-white flowers was popular, and each fragrant head in it was included for its own special significance.

Roses, symbolising faithfulness and enduring love, were considered essential: "They that would have beautiful roses in their gardens must have beautiful roses in their hearts."

Orange blossom for chastity and purity, and the lily of the valley symbolising "a return of happiness", were also part of the bouquet: as were sweetly-scented carnations, gardenias and waxy trumpets of stephanotis. The outer and final layer was usually of myrtle with its fragrant flowers and leaves, for that symbolised the evergreen eternal love that ought to distinguish marriage.

December

WEDNESDAY — DECEMBER 1.

I ONCE listened to an interesting radio talk by Roger Royle. He was speaking about the singing of hymns by those who are deaf or without the power of speech. An impossibility? Far from it.

He spoke of a Christmas Service held for deaf people in St Paul's Cathedral. I did not realise that you could "sing" hymns in sign language, and began to realise how poignant the carol "O Little Town Of Bethlehem" with a verse starting, "How silently, how silently the wondrous gift is given" must have been. It continues: "No ear may hear His coming . . ."

What a message here for all of us. If worshippers with serious disabilities can feel the love of God, how much simpler for the rest of us to appreciate it, surely.

THURSDAY — DECEMBER 2.

"I LIKE to keep myself to myself." We have all heard someone say this. And of course we all do need time and space to ourselves.

But we need other folk, too. People wrapped up in themselves make very small parcels.

SUNDAY — NOVEMBER 28.

THOU, O Lord, remainest for ever; thy throne from generation to generation.

Lamentations 5:19

MONDAY — NOVEMBER 29.

I HAVE friends who, to show their appreciation of moments of silence, turn off the radio and television at the end of an evening, and enjoy what they call "our silent half-hour". Several of their friends and neighbours are now doing the same thing.

William Penn, the religious leader who founded, and gave his name to, the American state of Pennsylvania, had this idea many years ago. "True silence," he said, "is the rest of the mind; it is to the spirit what sleep is to the body — nourishment and refreshment."

Many of us go into the sanctuary of a church just to find such moments of peace and quiet. Now, isn't it worth reminding ourselves that they can be created in our often busy and noisy homes as well?

TUESDAY — NOVEMBER 30.

NO matter how well we try to live our lives, there will be times when we exchange cross words with the ones we love. Regardless of what has been said, it's important to at least keep the lines of communication open.

Remember, you have to shout louder through a closed door.

FRIDAY — NOVEMBER 26.

THE SPIRIT WITHIN

WHEN the road lies dark before you
And it's hard to find the way,
Keep your spirit strong within you,
Hope will help you through each day.

When your worries overwhelm you
And the walls are closing in.
Seek that hidden strength inside you,
Feel a healing peace begin.

When the world looks vast and empty
And you're feeling quite alone,
Reach out for all your memories,
And the kindness you have known.

When you see a ray of sunshine
Never let it slip away,
Hold fast to all that you believe,
And you'll find a brighter day.

Iris Hesselden.

SATURDAY — NOVEMBER 27.

HERE is the briefest and probably the best description of the months of the year that I have ever seen:

Snowy, Flowy, Blowy,
Showery, Flowery, Bowery,
Moppy, Croppy, Droppy,
Breezy, Sneezy, Freezy.

It says it all, doesn't it?

RESTING
PLACE

WEDNESDAY — NOVEMBER 24.

A NOVEMBER item from one of Great-Aunt Louisa's diaries reads: "A soft grey, misty morning, there is nothing really wrong with me, yet I somehow feel a little fragile and in low spirits.

"However, I have just had a visit from a little friend as I write — my garden robin hopped into the kitchen through the back door which I had left open. Robins are such bright, perky, little birds.

"There is an old belief that if a robin comes indoors in November, it is a sign of good luck! You know, somehow I feel more cheerful already — self-pity is an indulgence surely not to be encouraged.

"This afternoon, I think I'll bake an orange cake from that favourite recipe given to me by Aunt Grace; David and Elsa will enjoy it when they come to tea tomorrow."

Beside this diary entry is a skilful little drawing of the robin and Great-Aunt Louisa looking at one another as if silently sharing a moment of friendship.

THURSDAY — NOVEMBER 25.

I LIKE the story of the little girl who was asked in Sunday school if she knew the story of Adam and Eve.

She replied, "First God made Adam, and then He looked at him and said, 'I think I can do better' — so then He created woman."

SUNDAY — NOVEMBER 21.

BUT let all those that put their trust in thee rejoice: let them ever shout for joy.

Psalms 5:11

MONDAY — NOVEMBER 22.

SO often we think life is about the big things — money, success and popularity. We perhaps tend to judge our lives by the success we see in others, and today that increasingly seems to mean show business stars and other such media personalities.

But one of life's great secrets is surely to celebrate the small — the sight of a flower growing between the cracks in a pavement, the look on a young child's face when they're given a birthday present they've waited for long weeks to open. Or something as simple as immersing ourselves in our favourite piece of music.

TUESDAY — NOVEMBER 23.

PATH OF HAPPINESS

SOMETIMES on the path of life
We tend to go astray,
With dark and hidden turnings
It's clear we've lost our way.
Then comes along a dear good friend
Who takes us by the hand,
Along the path of happiness
To a bright and hopeful land.

Jenny Chaplin.